The Large Sky Reaches Down

The Large Sky Reaches Down

---

*A statewide anthology
of Minnesota student writing
from the 1985–86 COMPAS
Writers & Artists-in-the-Schools
program*

Edited by
SUSAN MARIE SWANSON

Illustrated by
SUSAN NEES

COMPAS :: 1986

Publication of this book is made possible through the generous support of the Sven and C. Emil Berglund Foundation.

Copyright © 1986 by COMPAS Writers & Artists-in-the-Schools.
All rights reserved.
Cover Painting, "Crossing the Missouri" by Mary Griep, courtesy of MC Gallery.
No portion of this book may be reprinted or reproduced without the prior written permission of COMPAS.

COMPAS
Writers & Artists-in-the-Schools
308 Landmark Center
75 West Fifth Street
Saint Paul, Minnesota 55102
Molly LaBerge, Executive Director
Randy Jennings, Program Director

The title for this book is taken from a poem written by Charles McGuire, Cretin High School, St. Paul, during a residency with poet Sigrid Bergie.

The COMPAS Writers & Artists-in-the-Schools program is made possible by a grant from the Minnesota State Arts Board through an appropriation by the Minnesota State Legislature, and in part by a grant from the National Endowment for the Arts. Additional support is provided by the H. J. Andersen Foundation, the Jerome Foundation, the Jostens Foundation, the Otto Bremer Foundation and local school districts. COMPAS is a member agency of United Arts, and is the recipient of a McKnight Foundation award administered by the Minnesota State Arts Board.

Special thanks to teachers throughout Minnesota who sponsored COMPAS Writers & Artists-in-the-Schools residencies, and who nurture their students' creativity through the entire school year.

Thanks also to Carol Bergeland, Lisa Conley and Annette Jung in the COMPAS office, for all of the work they contributed toward preparing the manuscript and the book.

About COMPAS

COMPAS is the largest community arts agency in Minnesota, providing and sponsoring a variety of multi-disciplinary arts activities for people of all ages and abilities. Each year more than 150,000 Minnesotans enjoy and participate in COMPAS programs in schools, community centers, churches and businesses.

The COMPAS Writers & Artists-in-the-Schools program places professional writers and artists in elementary and secondary schools throughout the state, providing residencies in poetry, fiction, playwriting, visual art, music and theatre. During the 1985-86 school year over 32,000 students worked directly with COMPAS artists, learning from them the skills and techniques of particular disciplines.

At the conclusion of each school year representative student work from each of the writing residencies is selected and edited into an anthology of creative writing. *The Large Sky Reaches Down* is the 1986 COMPAS anthology, a celebration of the talents and vision of Minnesota students.

This book is a tribute to these student writers, and to the teachers, administrators, parents and artists whose efforts and dedication make the COMPAS Writers & Artists-in-the-Schools program a continuing success.

A Note to Teachers

The COMPAS Writers & Artists-in-the-Schools anthology celebrates the work done by the students participating in the 1985–86 program. The book also is intended to aid teachers in the teaching of creative writing. With this in mind, *The Large Sky Reaches Down* has been organized into thematic sections to allow teachers to find pieces on a particular topic or idea. This may make it easier to relate pieces of writing in the anthology to other activities in the classroom.

If there is a COMPAS writer in residence at your school, he or she can demonstrate how the anthology may be used in teaching. A good way to prepare students for a COMPAS residency is to read to the class from the anthology. Knowing that students their own age have published writing will spark interest and inspire confidence in the students' own writing.

A simple way to use these poems and stories as models for writing is to have students take a line, a title, or a subject from a piece of writing they like, to begin their own writing, and go on from there. Sharing the writing in the anthology can also help generate discussions about standards for writing: what makes a good piece of writing good? How can a weak piece be improved? How could an idea be expressed differently? All writers use other writers as models, and it is important that students know this. Using *The Large Sky Reaches Down* is an excellent way to demonstrate this process.

Table of Contents

INTRODUCTION: GIVING WHAT'S TRUE — *Susan Marie Swanson*

DANCING RAIN — *Normal Henderson*

Paradise Is So Close To Earth: The Sublime

"IF I STEPPED OUT OF MY BODY . . ."	*Justin LaDue*	2
"MY GRANDFATHER WAS A MOST CURIOUS MAN . . ."	*Sara Wilander*	3
AN EXPERIENCE TO REMEMBER	*James Carney*	4
THE FIGHTING ILLINI	*Jeff Jolley*	5
"WRINKLES ON THE FACE . . ."	*Tim Kelly*	6
IN MY DREAM	*Kim Pender*	6
HAVING FUN	*Andy Grimm*	7
THE CRICKET FROGS	*Brian Oehlke*	8
BIRDS	*Hoa Doan*	8
THE PIG	*Kim LaFave*	9
THE RAINBOW I SAW	*Mary Watts*	10
"THE FOLIAGE OF THE TOWERING TREES . . ."	*Polly Pemble*	11
MY VERY FIRST DAD	*Billy Jirovec*	12
I BROUGHT THEM INTO THE WORLD	*Mark Holmen*	13
"WE WOULD SMASH STYROFOAM . . ."	*Marc Nollette*	14
"LOVE IS SEEING YOUR FACE . . ."	*Kellie Rourke*	15
THE SAILBOAT ODE	*Cameron Chisholm*	16
THE WONDERFUL SHELL/ AN ODD SHELL	*Mark Rudnick*	17
HOW TO FLY	*Ryan Mahoney*	18
MY POEM	*Amy Toivonen*	19
GREAT GRANDMA	*Allison Wiley*	20
THE SILENCE OF CORN	*Jessica Johnson*	21

Then My Name Become Sorrow: Pain And Healing

HYAN WOO	*Nathan Stolt*	24
MY GRANDMA'S LOST CHILD	*Monica Moreno*	25
COLD HEART	*Angela Morse*	26
POEM ABOUT SILENCE	*Anette Nühse*	27
EXCERPT FROM "AT CANTURBURY DOWNS . . ."	*Jenny Hosford*	28
MILLY AND BOB	*Shawn Bagne*	29
NEW BUSINESS	*Cheryl Hennes*	31
WHY ME!!	*Dionne Wentland Mann*	32
MOTHERS	*Tracy Heinz*	33
REJECTED	*Cory Gustafson*	34
ANGER	*Harrison Grodnick*	35
A LETTER	*Mark Sampson*	36
MY BROTHER	*Kurt Christenson*	37
KOREA, 1975	*Mia Fjerstad*	38
FACES AND FEELINGS	*Sharon Koenig*	39
THE DEAD LEAF	*Andrea Knutson*	40
GRANDMA AND THE HUMMINGBIRD	*Sara Tyler*	41
BLEACHED BLACKNESS	*Dawn Syverson*	43
GRANDAD	*Eric Bangerter*	44
A LETTER TO MY MOM	*Craig Reedy*	45
YOU'RE ALWAYS HOME WITH ME	*Katie Richards*	46
THE LOON	*Katherine Ackerman*	47
GRANDPAW LEEK	*Jim Jones*	48

To Keep The World Alive: Words And Inventions

POETS	*Ryan Shirk*	50
THE TRICK	*John Jones*	51
BURNED EARS	*Becci Martin*	52
THE MASSACRE	*Heath Anderson*	53
MY SPECIAL CHANT	*Mike Johnson*	54
INSIDE A MARBLE	*Amy Boler*	55
"MY PENCIL IS A PLANT . . ."	*Steve Schelske*	56
LANGUAGE	*Shane Hepola*	57
THE PEN PAL	*Nate Hill*	58
SUGAR OR SUCRE: COFFEE SHOP IN QUEBEC	*Heather Shilling*	60
"I SEE THE LETTERS OF MY NAME . . ."	*Maggie Scanlon*	61

I GAVE AWAY MY HEART	*Matthew Danner*	62
GIVE IT AWAY	*Missy Tysver*	63
THE DREAM POEM	*Collaboration*	64
"I WAS WALKING . . ."	*Jay Apfel*	65
"THE ROARING WATERS OF THE CREEK . . ."	*Heidi Anderson*	66
BLACK CATS	*Scott Schaffer*	67
SPRING CLEANING	*Brandon Ulstad*	68
FLYING STARS	*Joe Oxendale*	69
DREAM TIME!	*Tara Otterbein*	70
CHANGES	*Kristine Fordham*	71
HOW COME, POET?	*Leann Okeson*	72
MR. SHOES	*Patrick Broderick*	73

MISSING A TOOTH: GROWING UP

"I'M MISSING A TOOTH . . ."	*Katy Mikrut*	76
HISTORY OF MY WRITING	*Jennifer Talcott*	77
A LETTER	*Jamie Miller*	78
THE CORN PEOPLE	*Shari Briley*	79
I REMEMBER	*Jack Shouts*	81
GROWING OLD	*Emily Larson*	82
OLD MOTOR OIL	*Stefan Reuther*	83
GARAGE ATTIC	*Mike Haugh*	84
THE FIRST SNOW	*Kris Kuehlwein*	85
REVIEW OF LIFE	*Robb Gag*	86
SCHOOL HALL FLOOR	*Troy Wallin*	87
WHAT LIFE IS ON SALE	*Ben Kuchera*	88
A NEW BASKET	*Sonia Tatroe*	89
FROM A BOY TO A GIRL	*Brandon Koontz*	90
SISTER	*Christine Touhey*	91
THE GIRL	*Keven Pellersels*	92
TEDDY	*Kim Haselius*	93
A LOSS	*Jodi Morgan*	94
MY BEDROOM	*Jenifer Schoeberl*	95
SISTER	*Wade Jensen*	96
GIFT	*Jerimy Erickson*	97
MY GREAT OLD UNCLE	*Howard Johnson*	98
THE FINAL DRAW	*Steve Munson*	99
CHICKEN	*Marjorie Ellickson*	100

DEVELOPMENT	*Rachel Weaver*	102
WE WALKED, WE RAN, WE FLEW	*Dave Parkin*	103

TO BE WITH THE WEATHER: NATURE AND SEASONS

TO BE WITH THE WEATHER	*Matthew Streit*	106
SEASONS	*Nichole Boegemann*	107
OATS IN A PAIL	*Sara Kubera*	108
THE SQUIRREL	*Eric Humble*	109
TRAPPED	*Jacinda Brinkman*	110
EXCERPT FROM "MY SPECIAL PLACE"	*Jennifer Timmer*	111
WORLD BEYOND MY HOME	*Laura Jasper*	112
ODE TO A SNOWSTORM	*Elliot Doren*	113
THE BLACK WINTER WATERS	*Ben O'Brien*	114
WINTER EXTRAVAGANZA	*Sara Rose*	115
SPRING	*Collaboration*	116
A LIKENESS	*Adrienne Feske*	117
ON SHREDDED WING	*Mark Olson*	118
DISTANCES OF NATURE	*Dan Knudson*	119
A PICTURE OF ME	*Shawn Clitty*	120
"FAITH WASN'T . . ."	*Melody Hanson*	121
"I SAW THE ROCK . . ."	*Tom Juenemann*	122
THE NATURE DAY	*Brian Sontag*	123
"I'M THE ONLY CHILD . . ."	*Tina Kassler*	124
GREAT-GRANDFATHER	*Greta Raduenz*	125
ESSENCE	*Amy Derr*	126
THE SHINTO GATES	*Chris Nordby*	127
THE DEER	*Sue Durand*	128

THE LARGE SKY REACHES DOWN: ON LIVING

VOLCÁN IRAZÚ	*Charles McGuire*	130
THE BEAMING LIGHT	*Adlai Czarnomski*	131
MOM	*Danae Meyer*	132
LAOS TO TAILAND	*Boonpheng Kavanh*	133
THE LIFE OF A DOWN'S SYNDROME CHILD	*Katie Eichten*	134
POEM WITH REFRAIN	*Bonnie Jo Snidarich*	136
"BILLY HOTCHKINS LOST HIS CAT . . ."	*Bryan Eggen*	137
SILENCE OF THE EARTH	*Chad Meiners*	139
LIFE	*Matt Schlotthauer*	139

THE SHARK	*Jon Shankland*	140
THE FIERCE LION	*Mandi Thoemke*	141
THE WAR	*Shawn Petersen*	142
WHEN THE MOON SAILS OUT	*Jenni Adams*	143
THE HAMMER	*Paul Welch*	145
KEEP ON LIVING	*Jodi Sommerfeld*	146
WINTER SKIN	*Che Regnier*	147
I WAKE UP AND REMEMBER	*Robert Atendido*	148
A TEACHER TAUGHT	*Tim Gustafson*	149
THE SUN	*Jason Moudry*	149
"I AM JUST A KID . . ."	*Jason Surface*	150
"BECAUSE OUR MINDS . . ."	*Tom Prow*	150
ODE TO THE PLANETS	*Bobby Withers*	151
"EVERY DAY THE SUN . . ."	*James Peeders*	153
DEER	*Adam Rislov*	154
MY FRIEND THE MOON	*Seton McCool*	155

Introduction

Giving What's True

Each piece of writing in this book celebrates a week when a COMPAS writer found the way to a school somewhere in Minnesota—in Long Prairie, perhaps, or St. Paul, in Fergus Falls, Stillwater, or Grand Rapids—and was met by the students who would write these and many other poems and prose pieces. This annual anthology of student writing is a landmark for all of us connected with the COMPAS Writers and Artists-in-the-Schools program. It represents the spirited, intense activity that goes on when students and their teachers welcome writers—and *writing*—into their classrooms.

I've often wished that more adults had shared things they really cared about with me when I was young. Young people like to see what there is to be excited about in the world, be it fossils, newspapers, hockey, painting, or star-gazing. Lessons and activities originating in enthusiasm can be most powerful. When we COMPAS writers go into schools, we are sharing something that matters to us very much.

Writing is a special means of learning and expression for us. It is part of the hopes we have for children, too. We share poems and stories with students, things written by famous and unsung authors, by adults and young people. When we use the writing of others to help students get started on writing projects of their own, we're guiding them in a practice familiar to creative adults: writers are forever getting inspiration from other writers.

As they write, students understand that writing is not merely a way to prove that you know something, it is vehicle for discovery, exploration, and growth. All of them are capable of turning language to such use. Many other stories, scenes and poems that you would love to read were written during COMPAS residencies over the course of the 1985–86 school year. And every COMPAS writer could tell you stories about achievements that cannot fit onto the pages of this book.

One day this spring during a residency in northern Minnesota, a teacher told me that a child had waved a poem at her with a sprightly "I think I've got a new hobby!" after one of my visits with their class. It was a pleasure to see that student's enthusiasm mirrored in the teacher — the flush of excitement on her face, and the quaver of delight and disbelief in her voice.

In another town, a high school boy was quite sure that writing was not for him. It was his classmates who persuaded him that poems could be made out of things *he* knew about, reading aloud what they were writing about their farms, families, and imaginings. On the third day of the residency, the boy came in with a vivid description of his father at the wheel of his truck. Indeed, he brought his truck-driving father along to the all-school reading the next night, to hear him read the poem to an audience.

A vital aspect of our work during COMPAS residencies is to help students see that the sources of expressive writing — memories, observations, metaphor, wishes — are known to all of us. Often we encourage them to seize the language that they use every day and give it a place in poetry or prose. A first grader named Cary McNamara from a Bemidji school wrote:

The air is sometimes warm and sometimes cold.
You breathe with it.
You can sing with it.
You can talk with it.

Once a person knows that they *already have* what it takes to write, and once they have a safe place to try it out, the results can be extraordinary.

Whenever I go to a school, I like to explain to the students that there is poetry all over the world, everyplace you could ever go. Stop and think about that for a minute: there are people who read and write poetry in Chile and Finland, in Vietnam, in Honduras, the Soviet Union, and Senegal, as well as in England and the United States. How does it ever happen that we suppose that there is nothing in poetry that would interest us?

I hope that both the adults and the young people who read *The Large Sky Reaches Down* see in its pages possibilities for themselves as writers. The various pieces of writing have been gathered up into sections, in part to present and underscore their diversity. In the section that opens the anthology, for example, Sara Wilander describes her love for grandfather by telling about a wooden spoon he once carved for her, while James Carney sets down a mysterious, beautiful account of meeting a grandfather who has died out on the frozen lake in the winter. Jeff Jolley carefully renders the old, familiar objects in the room where he watches television with his grandmother.

COMPAS writers are a small part of an environment that can — but often does not — encourage such daring and deeply-felt writing as you find in this book. We spend only a little while with Sara, James, Jeff, and the others. The work that teachers do with youngsters, the care of parents and friends — these count for more than our brief presence.

And yet a visiting writer is a catalyst for creative expression. We are grateful to teachers, administrators, parents, and community leaders who make our work with students around Minnesota possible and fruitful. Those who arrange our residencies in their schools do a lot of planning, fundraising, and persuading to make our work with young people and their teachers happen. We hope that this anthology will encourage people in efforts to nurture the expressive writing of children, teenagers, and teachers.

In a poem that she wrote for her child, the American Indian poet Roberta Hill Whiteman says that we must "give what's true and deep, from the original in ourselves." Because so many students from around Minnesota have done that kind of giving, you have this book.

Susan Marie Swanson
November, 1986

Dancing Rain

Come rain, we welcome you, so come
and do your spatter dancing.
Do your drumming
Do your tapdancing.
I will see my reflection.
Do your snake-dance.
Play your clear flute.
The mist is drifting.

Normal Henderson :: Grade 4
Crestview Elementary School :: Cottage Grove

Paradise Is So Close to Earth: The Sublime

"If I stepped out of my body . . ."

If I stepped out of my body
there would be peace the rest of my
life. It would be full of chaos at the
same time. There are cub scouts that have
matches in their pockets and they use them
for fires instead of flint, and there
are people who will kill for fire. Just
off the highway we could see the beautiful
shape of the earth and right there I realized
that I would never step out of my body. As
the coffee machine spurted, I was dreaming
about what it would be like in paradise.
Like being free from danger, free
from sin. It would be a wonderful time
to live in. While I was dreaming
I realized paradise is so close
to earth right now.

Justin LaDue :: Grade 9
Clarissa High School :: Clarissa

"My grandfather was a most curious man..."

My grandfather was a most curious man. He was comical but intellectual. Musical but modest. He was proud of his one hundred per cent Swedish background and of his Norwegian wife.

In the "good old days," as he used to say, there was hard work but Grandpa — no — he always found time for fun. Even when I was little and he was growing old, he found time to make spoons out of wood for me and tell stories.

I once had a cat, and I was inquiring of my most trusted friend Grandpa for a name. After a bit of thought and rejection of even the best of his names, I thought of it — the perfect name. I said, "Grandpa, I know — I'll call it Percy." I thought he'd be happy, but instead there was a grave look on his face. He said, "Don't call that poor kitten Percy. If you do, it will die."

Now, I was kind of a smart kid myself, and I couldn't quite believe him. So I went right ahead and named her Percy. Sure enough, I didn't even have her a whole summer, and she climbed up into the old maple tree and jumped out. I must say she died.

My grandfather made wooden spoons, and they were always just right. He never sold them, he always gave them away. My mother had quite a set of them, and to me and my new teeth they even tasted good. Every now and then I would take a spoon and chew on it. I got hearty spankings for that.

My grandpa loved to spoil me and hated to see me get into trouble. So he made me my own special little spoon to chew on. After that I didn't get spankings for that crime.

Over the years he made me a whole set that will always be special to me. I will treasure them forever, especially cherishing that first one.

My grandfather may have had his faults — being a little stubborn was one — but in my eyes he'll always be my perfect friend.

Sara Wilander :: Grade 7
Bemidji Middle School :: Bemidji

An Experience to Remember

It is winter up at the lake where my grandfather died.
The water is still frozen.
I see a man on the water:
he comes to me and looks vaguely familiar.
I notice a scar on his right hand.
I know now that he is my grandfather.
His white hair matches the white snow,
the white ice and his white breath.
I can see through him as though he were
a cloud, as though he were fog.
His face is worn with a look of happiness.
He touches me and starts to fade.
He is gone.
I turn around and walk away knowing
now that it is good wherever you go
after you die.

James Carney :: Grade 7
Breck Middle School :: Minneapolis

The Fighting Illini

I am sitting on a black recliner with
the piece of hockey tape over the rip.
We are in the living room . . . it's got
stained carpet and old furniture.
My grandmother sits on the couch
with the blanket that she made.
She takes a drink of her Budweiser
that sits next to the Lassie statue
with a broken tail.
We are watching the football game.
As I look at the door with all the bells
on it, I hear the fans cheering
on the football game.
In the background I can hear
the garage door opening and
my grandfather drive in. We watch
the football game often.
She loves the Fighting Illini football team.

Jeff Jolley :: Grade 5
Farmington Middle School :: Farmington

"Wrinkles on the face..."

Wrinkles on the face
indicate where smiles have been
on a happy man

Tim Kelly :: Grade 7
St. Thomas Academy :: St. Paul

In My Dream

I dream of wheat swaying like the ocean waves.
From the tallness of the wheat you will go in and get lost.
It feels like the wind going through my mind.
It looks like it is my kind.

Kim Pender :: Grade 4
Riverside Elementary School :: Moorhead

Having Fun

Jason is like a comedian up
    on stage entertaining
people, like a clown making people laugh
      until they cry.
    Jason Burns is like a cheetah
running so fast no one in 5th Grade
    can beat him.
      Jason Burns is like the obstacle
course burning because
        he's so quick.
      Jason is like a trumpet sounding
forth beautiful music to
    all the world.
    Throwing discs at him
is like sending flares to make
      Peace.

    The moral of this story is there's
never an end to *having fun.*

Andy Grimm :: Grade 5
Meadowbrook Elementary School :: Golden Valley

The Cricket Frogs

The cricket frog jumped on
my head then all of a sudden
a whole swarm of cricket
frogs jumped out from the hill
filled with flowers and the cricket
frogs ate me. On that moonlit
night I knew I would
never touch ground again.
I would have to live spiritually
the rest of my life.

Brian Oehlke :: Grade 6
Armstrong Elementary School :: Cottage Grove

Birds

On my summer shirt
birds fly around and around.
They don't seem to stop.

Hoa Doan :: Grade 4
Horace May Elementary School :: Bemidji

The Pig

The pig dreams about porkchops
                being killed
                going down a throat
                ending up in a deep dark stomach

but when it wakes up it finds itself by its mother's side
                                            getting kissed
                                            having brothers and sisters
                                            and being in pig heaven

Kim LaFave :: Grade 6
Buffalo Intermediate School :: Buffalo

The Rainbow I Saw

The rainbow I saw
was as interesting
as a dog shaped like a sock.

It came clear
after God had a long cry.

The colors were as bright
as fluorescent bracelets.

The rainbow was hanging in the sky
and it disappeared.

My sister is drawing it
with red, green, purple and blue markers.

Mary Watts :: Grade 3
Handke Elementary School :: Elk River

"The Foliage of the Towering Trees..."

The foliage of the towering trees provided perfect shading from the bright warmth shining above. A young girl lay across a footbridge on her back and bent her knees over the side to let her feet dangle in the cool rushing stream.

The clearing was a magical place for her to go to be all alone with her dreams. It was special because it was so secluded and unknown to others. The most beautiful time was at night when it was transformed into a mystical fairyland; the water glistened with a silvery light from the moon and the trees took on new startling personalities.

Now, the familiar figures stood with their arms outstretched as if to comfort and protect her. She closed her eyes and lovingly fingered the gold bracelet that hung on her wrist. She had worn it every day since the night she had gotten it because it meant so much to her.

Her thoughts were jolted back to reality with the pounding of feet running on the path nearby. She recognized the young, loud voices that followed, filled with harsh laughter.

She scrambled up and ran to the other bank to get away. She felt the familiar weight slip from her wrist and hesitated, not knowing whether to stop and look for the bracelet. As she glanced around, hoping her eye would catch the sparkle of gold, the voices grew louder and closer, and she ran on.

Polly Pemble :: Grade 9
Stillwater Junior High School :: Stillwater

My Very First Dad

My first dad,
I remember him when I go to
Texas, like god in my heart.
I remember him in my heart
like clouds overhead,
and strawberry ice cream and bananas
when I was a little kid. But the most
I remember is his love,
as big as Texas
when I was born.

Billy Jirovec :: Grade 5
Newport Elementary School :: Newport

I Brought Them Into The World

I was born August 4, 1971.
By the age of 7, I was Dad's little helper on the farm.
One night Dad woke me up at 1:00 a.m. and told me to get
   dressed
We then trudged through many feet of snow to reach
the hoghouse.
Another batch of tiny, pink piglets, but
the pigs were trapped inside the sow, because the first pig
was twisted inside.
I was instructed to enter the pen, with the help of my father,
and pull the piglets, because my hands were smaller.
I cried and cried, scared to enter the pen, because that
sow was mean.
But I was finally urged on to success.
I did it. In front of me lay 10 healthy, pink piglets,
struggling to survive, not in the sow, but
in the bright, warm, new world.

Mark Holmen :: Grade 8
Lanesboro High School :: Lanesboro

"We would smash styrofoam . . ."

We would smash
styrofoam rose covers
that would keep dainty
roses warm during the
winter months.
We would lob eggs off
a broken railroad tie
that hung over a gloomy
north shore line bridge.
Those were the days.
I can remember when all
we would do was go out
and not be seen until
the light was dark
and eveyone yawned as we
looked at each other's wrinkled,
baggy eyes,
drooping faces.
By the time the Milwaukee
sky was turning black,
we would have the city
turned up on end.
The days have long since
passed.
While we talk, they seem
to rush on like the brisk
wind that carries winter.
Now, all grown up, looking
back, we see the roses
are uncovered and growing in
the sun that feeds them.

Marc Nollette :: Grade 11
Rosemount High School :: Rosemount

"LOVE IS SEEING YOUR FACE . . ."

Love is seeing your face in
a stream of pearls, with a view of
a cardinal sitting proud on a
oak branch behind you.
Love is you dancing to the sound
of a flute in the background of
my dream. You light up a fall
night with your love and grace
as we watch deer run swift and
graceful, the moon shining down
on us bright and beautiful,
while a violin plays our favorite
tune softly. You are the one who
helps me love my life and for
that I thank you.

Kellie Rourke :: Grade 6
Zanewood Elementary School :: Brooklyn Park

The Sailboat Ode

Gracefully sailing through the sea
like a bar of wet soap skidding
across the counter. Red and
green like the markers
on my desk. Finding its
way from the wind. At
night when the wind is
still, it follows the stars
until it gets to land.

Cameron Chisholm :: Grade 4
Ada Elementary School :: Ada

The Wonderful Shell

It is like a stairs going up to heaven. With angels guarding the way up the tremendous stairs. When you look up all you can see is a big flash of light. With brown and a wonderful beige white.

An Odd Shell

It is rather small, about the size of a peanut. It is light pink with a chalky looking white. It feels like a rose stem. Pokey but beautiful. The inside is like a ripple in the middle of a calm pond that a kid threw a rock in. It never stops.

Mark Rudnick :: Grade 6
Fergus Falls Middle School :: Fergus Falls

How to Fly

Take bird feathers
    and a little fire from the sun,
Take some pine needles
    and a young cloud,
Take some air (just a little)
    and don't forget rain.

Put it all in a bowl,
    stir it up and drink it
And find the highest mountain
    and jump.

Ryan Mahoney :: Grade K
Lincoln Elementary School :: South St. Paul

My Poem

A poet uses words as much
as a balloon uses air.
A poet uses words as long as
you can hold your breath.
A poet uses as many words as
he or she can think of.
A poet uses so many words
that they cannot remember what words
they have already used!
But the more words the poem uses,
it gets better and better.
Otherwise a poet is stingy
and gets frustrated,
doesn't like the poem,
drops it in the garbage —
and that was the poem
that shone like the sun.

Amy Toivonen :: Grade 4
Southwest Elementary School :: Grand Rapids

Great Grandma

I want to speak for
my great grandma
who would make my heart
spark, with a wooden
cane black as coal.
She put a smile on
my face with her
dark warm eyes.
Her face always glowing
and waiting for a visit.
Great grandma had stringy
gray hair standing out
like a flame. Her
eyes twinkled and
sparkled like diamonds
and her fingers felt
like gold but now
all I have to
remember her by is
her last words,
"I'll always be. . . . "
and her picture.

Allison Wiley :: Grade 4
Osseo Elementary School :: Osseo

The Silence of Corn

Silence is like a sprout of green corn
taking its own time to come out of the ground.
After it grows as tall as me, the cob will come
silent as a prowling cat about to pounce.
When it turns the soft yellow of a baby's blanket,
we will come and pick it.
After we get home, we boil it to make the house
smell like Mom is baking fresh bread.
Then we will eat it.
In spring, we plant more corn
so we can wait for it to grow again,
sprouting silently
like a little ballerina dancing away.

Jessica Johnson :: Grade 5
Norman County West Elementary School :: Hendrum

Then My Name Became Sorrow:
Pain and Healing

Hyan Woo

My name started with a rain cloud
Its name was Hyan Woo
As it started across Korea it burst
Down came my name
In a shape of a raindrop
My name landed on my father
My father was drunk
Without thinking he gave it to me
My name was in the streets
My name meant joy as my father drew
pictures for people
Then my name became sorrow
Sorrow, for our mother had left us
Sorrow, for I left my father
Then my name changed
as I crossed the seas
It became Nathan.

Nathan Stolt :: Grade 7
New Ulm Junior High School :: New Ulm

My Grandma's Lost Child

A baby crawls to its mother's arms
and before it gets there
it disappears

And holding me tight was Grandma
with a sad face.
Her face turned red.
She wouldn't let me go, she thought
my uncle, her lost child,
was me.
At night she would cry herself to sleep.
And wouldn't eat and all that time
she had me in her arms
because

Before it got to her
her child disappeared.

Monica Moreno :: Grade 7
Mankato East Junior High School :: Mankato

Cold Heart

When I was seven years old my
brother died. My expression
was like when a window
has been broken by the
cold winter. And the people
who lived there couldn't
pay for the broken window.
So they had a boy that
was ten years old who had
cancer and passed away.
So all their lives they
had a cold spot in their
heart.

Angela Morse :: Grade 6
Tanglen Elementary School :: Hopkins

Poem About Silence

When I am sad
my brothers shield me
like a witch her magic book.

They take me in their arms,
and I can feel the silence of friendship
kept deep inside them.

A mute feeling pervades me
like helium filling a balloon.
Nothing has to be said
between my brothers and me
We feel the silence in our souls,
the love in our hearts.

Anette Nühse :: Grade 12
Glenville High School :: Glenville

Excerpt from "At Canterbury Downs . . ."

(At Canterbury Downs — Jennifer and Gina)

J: That horse is pretty isn't it?

G: Yeah. So what.

                (Pause.)

J: I like working as a stable girl.

G: It's OK.

J: I really like the horse Sugarfoot over in the other barn.

G: Just be quiet and leave me alone.

J: Why should I leave you alone when you're my partner. You're supposed to help me, not order me around.

G: I told you to leave me alone.

J: Why? Are you mad?

G: NO!

J: Then why should I leave you alone?

G: My mother died yesterday . . .

Jenny Hosford :: Grade 6
Roosevelt Elementary School :: South St. Paul

Milly and Bob

Setting: A cafe. Four tables with table cloths, a window with a curtain and a bright overhead light. A clear window for a snack bar. A cash register, gum ball machines, coat hangers, fans, and sixteen chairs.

MILLY Can I take your order?

BOB Yeah, I'll have a hot dog and milk, then a pizza and two donuts.

MILLY Will that be all?

BOB Yes.

MILLY It will be ready in a moment.

BOB Sure, it will probably take two hours.

MILLY How come you're mad all the time?

BOB Just this morning a boy stole ten dollars from me!

MILLY Don't be so angry, it was only ten dollars.

BOB Only ten dollars!

MILLY Do you have a wife?

BOB No, she passed away. Ever since I've been mad and sad.

MILLY Do you have any friends?

BOB No.

MILLY   You are a pretty nice guy when you get to know you.

BOB   Do you really mean it?

MILLY   Yes, in fact, I kinda like you.

BOB   Really?!

MILLY   I'm going to go check on your food.

BOB   She is a nice lady, I must say.

MILLY   (Bringing the food) Your food is ready. Here is your hot dog, milk, pizza, and two donuts.

BOB   I think you have made me come to my senses. Thank you. You are one great lady.

Shawn Bagne :: Grade 4
Probstfield Elementary School :: Moorhead

New Business

We wait in the rain after school
    for an hour,
        my sister and I.
The sky spatters the merry-go-round.
Like the playground, I am silent.

        An apologetic Mom finally arrives.
        "It's the business," she explains.

In a noisy shop's back room
    we while away the time,
        my sister and I.
Amid the presses' roar I remember
how it used to be.

        Mom was always there. But now,
        "It's the business," she explains.

At home we are wide eyed
    and wondering
        my sister and I.
Our thoughtless play stops when
we hear the sobs from the bedroom.

        Sobs from a mother who never cried.
        Later—"It's the business," she explains.

Cheryl Hennes :: Grade 11
Osseo Senior High School :: Osseo

Why Me!!

Last year towards the end of the school year, I went home after school with my brother. We got off the bus and started walking up our dirt driveway. I noticed both my parents were home. I went inside and my mom was in her bedroom wallpapering. The wallpaper was white with little blue flowers all over that remind me of paw prints. My mom seemed mad when I went in to say "Hi." Then she said, "Dionne, we have to have a talk." I was really scared, trying fast to think of what I had done wrong so I could think of an excuse while at the same time my stomach felt like there were butterflies inside. She took me to the kitchen table where I sat with my back to the sliding glass door. My mom sat with her back to the counter facing my dad, and my brother facing me. My mom said, "Go ahead Frank, tell them." My dad tried to talk but he started to cry. He grabbed some napkins from the table to wipe his tears. I had never ever seen my dad cry before in my whole life. So many things went through my head, I thought of what if one of them had a disease, or what if my dog died, or my grandma or grandpa, then I thought of what if they were going to get a divorce. That was it. I tried so hard not to cry. I grabbed a napkin and covered my face as I yelled, "Tell me what's wrong!" My dad started to talk in a stuttered, whimpering voice. He said, "Your mother and I have decided to get a divorce." My brother was only nine and he yelled, "NO!" and ran to his room. By this time my mom was crying and I had never before had the feeling that I had then. I felt so sorry for my brother because he didn't really know how to take it. My whole family was crying except me. I held it in as hard as I could, then I muttered out, "Can I leave now?" My mom said, "Yes." As soon as I stood up from my chair which was sticking to my legs because I had shorts on, I yelled, "I HATE YOU, WHY DOES THIS HAVE TO HAPPEN TO ME, WHY!!" I yelled as loud as I could, ran to my room and stuffed my face under my pillow and cried. Tears ran down my cheeks and it tickled. My mom came into my room and I yelled, "GET OUT!"

Dionne Wentland Mann :: Grade 7
Salk Junior High School :: Elk River

MOTHERS

Now look what you did, you broke the glass don't you know how to do anything. That's the way it always is, can't you do anything right. I think that's all she says. Her other line is do this do that and get it done now! I tell her every time I already did that and I didn't break it. Once she told me you better get your life together or else. I said to her or else what. She didn't say anything it just went to silence. Then all at once she goes how dare you say that. Say what. You know what. Well I don't do all the things you say I do, and why should I clean up after the pigs in the family. And that's all I heard out of her.

Tracy Heinz :: Grade 6
Hanover Elementary School :: Hanover

Rejected

Big, sturdy and strong . . . alone.
As I wait and remember, about being
stuffed in a sack with twelve of
my kind and two heavy bricks.
The ride that seemed forever.

And our volley over the
bank and into the dark wetness.
My muzzle found a hole in the
sack; I ripped for my life.
. . . I was washed up on shore.

I live by killing not only
for food but because of the
pain of being rejected.

I am now a wild dog.

Cory Gustafson :: Grade 6
Franklin Middle School :: Thief River Falls

Anger

One day when I was
going to my
friend's house I saw my anger
come up to me,
and it said *I'm leaving
you*, but I didn't want him to.
So I begged him
and begged him, but he said
*No. You use me too
much*, and I said *Well I
won't — I can't
help it.*
But he walked away.
That night when I was asleep I heard my
anger walking downstairs in
to the kitchen. It
opened the refrigerator
and started to eat.
Then I came downstairs
while he was drinking a pop
and eating a peanut butter sandwich. And
I said *What are you doing*, and he
said *Eating* and ran. I put on
my clothes
and tried to catch him,
but he was too fast for me,
so I tried to catch him on my
bike, and when I got really close
to him he just vanished. So I
went home
without my anger but that

night he came back
to me and I was really glad.

Harrison Grodnick :: Grade 4
Katherine Curren Elementary School :: Hopkins

A Letter

Dear Dad,

After last night's fight,
my heart is split in half with apologies.

When I look at a cloud, I see you and
me with fire between us. I hope the flames
create a dove.

I'm sorry I fought with my sister.
My brain must be in the shape of a fist.

I saw a star in the sky in the form of a heart.
I hope it's a sign of the future for you and me.

Mark Sampson :: Grade 8
Valley View Junior High School :: Edina

My Brother

My brother jumps up
and is no longer a person.
But a black-winged cardinal
soaring over the trees.
Switching sadness to happiness
never noticing the wild madman.
And with the blink of an eye
soars over the cloudy dark skies.
And takes a deep breath
and blows
and instantly the sky is
blue and the sun shines like
a ruby.
Then he swoops down
and turns into himself.

Kurt Christensen :: Grade 4
Shirley Hills Elementary School :: Mound

Korea, 1975

I was born in Korea, 1975.
Then was given up on the sidewalk in Seoul.
It was cold and lonely.
Until the police came
and put me in a foster home.
Then I was adopted in 1977.
I drove my new parents into space.
And even broke a vein in my mom's wrist.
I was having health problems.
Pretty soon I had to get ready for —
the big operation.
It was my heart.
Doctors said after my operation
I would still be a vegetable.
In Korea there was a church praying
for me.
500 people there were.
Pretty soon I got out of the hospital.
And because of the people in Korea
I was healed.
The years passed,
and at the age of 10 the doors of
heaven really opened up to me.
I started to learn how to really
worship God.
And my life
was filled with more happiness.

Mia Fjerstad :: Grade 4
Grove City Elementary School :: Grove City

Faces and Feelings

My family has never been
a picture family.
I love to take pictures
to remember things,
a special event,
a candid moment,
or just to remember
how someone looked.
I wish we had albums
of faces and feelings,
so I could see
what my family was like.
I'll never know
what I looked like
as a baby.
I never met my Grandma Newman
and I'll never know
what she looked like.
Her death
was too painful
for my grandfather,
and the few photos
taken of my grandmother
perished in the flame
started by his tears.
Nothing can stop time
like a photograph,
and I wish my family
had wanted
to stop time.

Sharon Koenig :: Grade 10
Swanville High School :: Swanville

The Dead Leaf

Joan threw her pillow onto the floor. The clock read 3:06 a.m. She couldn't sleep. She got up out of her blue satin sheets. Looking around she saw her old clown doll. With just the light from her clock she looked closely at the tear in the arm which her younger sister had made while they were fighting two years ago. Her closet door was partly open revealing her clothes which her sister had begged to wear almost every day. Joan had always refused though. Joan looked on her dresser at the make-up she had received from her sister. A tear rolled off Joan's eye as she walked over to the open window. A leaf fell and rested on the window sill. She picked it up. It was a brown, dry leaf. It was dead. Just like her sister. She couldn't stand this any longer. She picked up the doll lying on a chair next to her bed. It was the one her sister had given her. It had light golden hair and big blue eyes. On the other side of the bed was a nightstand with her favorite lamp her grandmother had given her. It was to be given to the first born child. She remembered how her sister envied her for getting it. Now she wished her sister would have gotten it. She could also remember the times when they had fought over small things. Like the gold chain on her dresser which she had found in the attic. She slowly moved from her bed and pulled on her bathrobe. She wanted to get out of her room, her memories were making her feel guilty. She walked over to the door and reached out for the knob.

As she walked down the dark, lonely hallway, she stopped and looked at their family's pictures on the wall. She looked at the one of her and her sister in their Halloween costumes three years ago. Joan had always disliked that picture but now it meant more to her. As she moved down the hall, she noticed a box full of her sister's toys. To the left of that was an old rolltop desk and chair. She sat down at it and took out a pencil and paper. She started making a list of all the things she would have done if her sister were still alive. Some of the things she wrote were: teach her how to pitch a softball, help her wash her hair when she asked. Two tears rolled down her cheeks. She threw the paper into the desk and closed the cover with a bang. She ran through the hall and slammed her bedroom door. She didn't care if she woke her parents, she just wanted her sister back.

Andrea Knutson :: Grade 6
Birch Grove Elementary School :: Brooklyn Park

GRANDMA AND THE HUMMINGBIRD

One day she was gone.
Grandma was gone.
Her face is a china doll,
it follows me everywhere I go.
Then one night her face faded.
I heard her voice,
she said I must go.
I cried.
She was gone.
An angel with big beautiful wings
and a harp took her away.
She was gone,
gone forever.
Sometimes I see an angel,
that angel has her face.
Then a year ago it disappeared
as a hummingbird.
Some nights,
that hummingbird comes back.
It hurts.
Fills my head with the smell
of her perfume.
That hummingbird's hum is there.
It always will be.

Forever and ever.
Making me cry.
It hurts.
Fills my eyes with tears.
I cry.
She's gone.
Gone forever and ever.
The hum is here,
it will be forever.
She's gone.
The bird's here.

Sara Tyler :: Grade 4
Knox Elementary School :: Thief River Falls

Bleached Blackness

           Black.
The wrinkled, calloused hands
    Are permanently stained
      A fifty-year
           Black.
     Steel shapers
Molding the horse metal
  To a perfect fit;
      Permanently stained
        Black.
     Persistent demands
Require relentless resolution
    And steadfastness.

        Slowly
   the demands diminish.
        Slowly.
    Until one day
      the black
      fades away
     Permanently.
     Permanently.

Dawn Syverson :: Grade 12
Willmar Senior High School :: Willmar

GRANDAD

Your name
was sick,
a clock waiting to wind
down.
Your name
was a rusted engine,
waiting to get fixed.
Now your name
is better,
an old clock being rewound.
Your name
is a well-tuned engine,
purring away.
Your name
is a piece of wood,
but it was carved into
a bird.
Then painted to perfection.
Your name
is alive.
Life itself.

Eric Bangerter :: Grade 6
Alice Smith Elementary School :: Hopkins

A Letter to my Mom

Mom,

    When you were in the hospital I went to heaven and talked to God and we decided that it was time for you to die.

    And every night I sat on a rainbow and thought, and the other day I hurt my knee but I thought of you and it made me feel good.

    Yesterday Mom, I wasn't going to tell you this, but I went to Never Land and met a Pegasus and he took me home because it was time for bed.

    Mom, one more thing, I have to tell you this. I think of unicorns and pegasuses and birds, especially I think of love because it mostly reminds me of you.

Craig Reedy :: Grade 3
Birch Grove Elementary School :: Brooklyn Park

You're Always Home With Me

The small ghost-like image
jumps through the soft wind. He turns
to question me. He seemed to say there
is no way home. My home is like
a bowl of love which I miss so bad. I
nodded and he seemed to say
you're always home with me.

Katie Richards :: Grade 5
Shirley Hills Elementary School :: Mound

The Loon

During the night the clouds had sunk down onto the still lake of glass. The mist swirls in silent eddies like a swarm of regal ghosts walking from place to place in silver ribbony paths. One can hear the conversation of drops of water on leaves. It is the sound of utter silence ringing in my head. From the depths of the mist a single tone begins as an unconscious song. The note swells, it is everywhere and nowhere. Suddenly it breaks to a higher pitch, wailing from the mist, from my heart. It fades slowly, disperses, then it is gone. I had heard the cry released from the snowy soul of a lonely spirit, a cry of beautiful despair, the cry of the wilderness.

Katherine Ackerman :: Grade 10
Mounds Park Academy :: St. Paul

GRANDPAW LEEK

Remembering calling him Grandpaw Lake.
When we would fish, gosh
if he caught a fish he would say
"It's not the one." He would just talk
about the walleye, the so-called 25 pounder.
I would think when he would die,
his veins so brittle with
the gentle breeze. And when the sun
was just rising at 6
the golden lake and the green algae
looking so green. Then when gazing out, his pole went down
he said "Oh God, I've got it."

Jim Jones :: Grade 7
Oltman Junior High School :: St. Paul Park

To Keep the World Alive: Words and Inventions

Poets

Being a poet is easy.
The pages turn in your head —
like lightning.
Comets whiz
and the world turns.
The pencil is magic.
Your thoughts are about to burst
The words fly by like eagles
and they slide right into place.
When you're done with the poem
the pages stop turning.
The comets are gone
and the world stops turning.
The pencil dies
and the words aren't flying.
And now I'll write another poem
to keep the world alive.

Ryan Shirk :: Grade 5
Westview Elementary School :: Apple Valley

The Trick

When I was with my granddad
feeding up the cows we saw DEATH.
He was wearing a red suit and a red
Chinese hat. He had a long sharp stick.

When he saw us he jumped up in the
air, and landed in front of me and my
granddad. Where he stood he burned the
hay and barley. Then I had a plan. I would have
to trick him. So I said there's a ghost in
back of you. So he looked in back of him.

Then me and my granddad grabbed the
hose and we put water on him. He burned
and steamed like water on a stove. Then he disappeared
and turned into a cardinal and flew away.
And that's how I tricked DEATH.

John Jones :: Grade 6
Glen Lake Elementary School :: Minnetonka

Burned Ears

My ears are bored.
All day they've heard
    the droning monotone of teachers' voices,
    the shrill screaming of my mother.
And so,
one night they deserted me.
They laughed gleefully at the trick they'd played.
They traveled on airy wings to rolling green hills,
heard the winds' soft moans,
the eagles flying overhead,
the swish of their wings.
They flew to the big city,
heard the voices of angry cars.
They ran, freezing, to a neighbor's house
to warm their bodies by the fire.
But alas, they got too close
and burned their wings.
They couldn't come back to me.
I never heard the alarm this morning.
I never will.

Becci Martin :: Grade 12
Long Prairie High School :: Long Prairie

The Massacre

I am the writer
Who seeks to find freedom.
   When I write it is like slaughtering
the wind that crawls upon me!

It is like flogging the souls that feed
upon me!

It is grinding the rust that grows
upon my legs!

It is to demolish the evil that seeks to
find me!

It is catching and slaying the men who
forget me!

When I finish my art I shall set it to
freedom!

Heath Anderson :: Grade 4
Callaway Elementary School :: Detroit Lakes

My Special Chant

I had a bike with wings of silver
that flew me all over

I had a jacket with built-in muscles
that made me the strongest boy in the world

I had a rainbow captured in a jar
that made me smile the best smile

I had a gun that shot money
I had a fish that laid candy eggs
I had a dog with gold hair
I had a big monster that ate everything I had.

Mike Johnson :: Grade 4
Washington Elementary School :: Moorhead

Inside a Marble

Being inside a marble is like walking
in a city of glass and lights. For the
colors are like lights or rainbows.
It's as smooth as fingernails and as fun
as an amusement park. When someone
rolls the marble I feel like I am riding
a roller coaster. I get dizzy and the colors
blend together. The marble hits a wall,
it cracks and soon I'm outside.

Amy Boler :: Grade 6
Tilden Elementary School :: Hastings

"My pencil is a plant . . ."

My pencil is a plant
that grew from the ground.
It talks to my paper silently.
It is an obstacle
that works by my fingertips.
It is a spider with one leg
creeping down my paper.
It is a part of my body
that speaks its own language.

Steve Schelske :: Grade 7
Taylors Falls School :: Taylors Falls

LANGUAGE

My grandma speaks Finnish.
She talks very fast.
I don't know what she is talking about.
She is afraid of the word "Death."
My two grandmas talk to each other.
They talk to me.
I have to remind them to talk
to me in English.
They say oh yes, I forgot.

Shane Hepola :: Grade 5
Deer Lake Elementary School :: Bemidji

The Pen Pal

One day Henry wrote a "pen pal" letter to his friend Sven in Germany.

"This is going to be fun!" Henry exclaimed. Henry finished hurriedly and ran out the door in record time. He ran down Seventh Street, turned at Suburban Road and stopped at the mailbox, jumped up and down excitedly and dropped the letter in the box and left.

About two weeks later he received the letter back again. He looked at the letter curiously, then, he turned it over and looked. Henry noticed someone stamped "incorrect address." Henry turned the letter over again.

"Oh darn! I put the wrong address on the envelope," said Henry madly.

Well, Henry was very upset about this. He opened the envelope and took out the letter. Henry placed the letter in another envelope, wrote the address and checked the address fifty times.

Henry ran back to the mailbox and put the letter in the box and ran home.

OK fine, Henry put the right address on the envelope, unfortunately another problem came up. Sven could speak English but he couldn't write and read it.

About 7 months after he mailed the letter, Henry wondered what happened, so he wrote another letter to Sven to find out why he didn't write back.

When Sven received the letter, he couldn't think of anything else to do, so he wrote Henry back in German.

Translated into English, this is what Sven wrote:

Dear Henry,
    I'm almost sure you won't be able to read this so I'll keep it short. I can't read English!
                                  Your Pen Pal
                                       Sven

Then Sven mailed the letter.

Later in the U.S. Henry got the letter. "I got a letter! I got a letter!" Henry sang skipping around the house.

"Would you shut up?" yelled Henry's sister Harriet.

"I got a letter," said Henry smartly. Henry ran to the living room, plopped himself on a sofa and read the letter (attempted to read it anyway). When Henry saw the letter he just about cried. He slammed the letter on the couch and darted up to his room.

"I've never seen anyone get so emotional over a pen pal letter," said his mother.

Henry's dad sighed and went up to talk to Henry. When Bill (Henry's dad) arrived upstairs he knocked on the door.

"Come in," Henry said flatly.

"Henry, I know you're upset about the letter but most countries have their own languages, like the United States, where we speak English. In some cases at least two countries speak the same language — like Austria and Switzerland speak German.

"German?" Henry murmured. "German sounds like Germany. Is that what Sven wrote in?"

"Yes it is. Tell ya what. Let's go to Pickwick and get a German to English, English to German dictionary so you can read the letter and continue writing back to him," said Bill.

"All right!" Henry cheered. And from then on Henry and Sven have been good *pen pals*.

Nate Hill :: Grade 5
Mississippi Creative Arts School :: St. Paul

Sugar or Sucre: Coffee Shop in Quebec

I was rather disappointed to learn that I did not even need a passport to cross the border between the United States and Canada. We were in Quebec; I pronounced it "kay-beck" like my first year French teacher had at school. Being so worldly and well-traveled gave me a near tangible sense of maturity.

We sat in a restaurant. No, it was more like a coffee shop. On the red and white checked plastic table cloth was the typical coffee shop rack of sugar packets. Each package showed a scenic view of Canada's wilderness on one side and two words on the other — "sugar" and "sucre."

I reeled off as many French names of food as I could remember: beurre-butter, lait-milk, cafe-coffee.

At the next table, three men were speaking French. Logically, I knew that their conversation was private, and had nothing to do with the other people in the restaurant. I could not shake the feeling, though, that they were talking about us — that American family.

At a time when fitting in, being part of a group, was foremost in one's mind, how you looked — your shell — was less important than only one thing: what others thought and said of you. My adolescent paranoia was derived from the knowledge that since one gossiped incessantly about others, they were also probably talking about you.

I resumed my list of French nouns: forchette-fork, serviette-napkin, tasse-cup.

Heather Shilling :: Grade 12
Saint Paul Academy :: St. Paul

"I SEE THE LETTERS OF MY NAME . . ."

I see the letters of my name,
a design engraved by the many cracks
upon a turtle's green and black shell,
the writing delicate and elegant,
painstakingly carved by an unknown artist.

I carefully approach the small turtle,
reach down to scoop him out of the sand.
It does not attempt to flee from my grasp
but rather welcomes me as a friend.
I touch the hard dry shell,
and my name remains.
I put the turtle in a pail
and fold the net over the opening.

Later, I remove the net
and lay the pail on its side.
The turtle hesitates,
and then it slowly moves
into the light where my name
can be plainly seen by anyone
who cares to look.

There is where the turtle remained.
It moved no further
than the warm sand and sunshine
of the beach where it was found.

Maggie Scanlon :: Grade 10
Convent of the Visitation High School :: Mendota Heights

I Gave Away My Heart

Once I saw a pretty girl crying so I gave
her my heart so she will be happy. In return
she gave me a cobra. Oh do I wish I had my heart.
I lie on the ground now helpless. So please
don't ever give away your heart. Give them
love.

Matthew Danner :: Grade 3
Adams Elementary School :: Fergus Falls

Give It Away

In the evening
I gave my heart
away, the sun came
back like a blazing
horse. In the morning I
gave my love away, the
moon came back like
a silver egg. At midnight
I gave away a dove, and
a piece of silk came back.
At sunset I gave my ears
away, and a red rose
came back. At dawn
I gave my nose away,
and a blue jay came back
with a worm in its mouth.

Missy Tysver :: Grade 3
McKinley Elementary School :: Fergus Falls

The Dream Poem

Between falling asleep and waking up
I dream of going to school and not working.
I dream that tomorrow I'll get presents and give them.
I dream I'll call my dog "Scooter".
I dreamed a brown and pink lion was chasing me.
I knew it wasn't real.
I was as scared as a spookhouse.
I was running like a blue dog after the ham that escaped from
    the plate.
When I dreamed I was a lightbulb
it was like being a piece of yellow paper hanging over a can
    opener in Korea.
In my dream the snow was as deep as a glass of milk beside
    the sunflowers and rose thorns.
In my dream they called me "cheese of the cat."
They called my sister "Tanya the dog."
My mom was the bird and my dad was the cage of the bird.
It was March 27th and as cold as light night's pizza.
In the morning my imagination shut off like a radio and I
    couldn't find the knob to turn it back on again.

Collaboration :: Grade 1
Southwest Elementary School :: Grand Rapids.

"I WAS WALKING . . ."

I was walking down a dusty country road. The sun's rays poured down on me and perspiration rolled down my back. My short brown hair was matted on my head. My green shirt and shorts were stuck to my body. The suitcase I was carrying felt like an elephant was in it. I looked over in a dry cornfield and saw a periscope sticking out of a hole in the ground. I cautiously walked over to investigate. As I peered down into the deep hole where the periscope was coming from, someone or something pushed me in. When I landed on the bottom, I slowly looked up. The cornfield seemed to be a million miles away. Then I saw it. A huge, three-legged creature. It hobbled over to me and locked me up in a dungeon. I tried to escape, but I couldn't, I was trapped.

Jay Apfel :: Grade 5
Folwell Elementary School :: Rochester

"THE ROARING WATERS OF THE CREEK . . ."

The roaring waters of the creek under the little wooden bridge smelled of strong fish and soggy trees. The water was a brown overlapping some green. I heard the ducks in the background, calling to each other. I could hear the buzzing cars bumpity-bump bump over the highway bridge behind me. And suddenly, he appeared. An old man, wearing tattered and torn rags with a worn-out hat. It looked as if he hadn't shaved for weeks with his dingy, white beard and dirty, grimy face. As I watched him, I became even more fascinated. He was trying to catch the over-fed carp in the water. He used his hands for they were all he had. He kept clapping and splashing around and saying vulgar words under his breath. I began to laugh with amusement. He was startled and looked up, I turned away quickly. When I thought it was safe, I slowly turned my neck to peek. But, when I looked, he had disappeared as quickly as he appeared before.

Heidi Anderson :: Grade 9
Oakland Junior High School :: Lakeland

Black Cats

Charley the black cat
had bad luck all of his
life.
He couldn't walk to
the neighbors' without
walking under
a ladder.
And when he was
done eating turkey
and brought the
wishbone to his
friend's house
he lost.
And when he was
combing his
fur
in the mirror
he sneezed
so hard
SMASH!!!
Oh No, seven years bad
luck!
And so he bought a horseshoe
and he dropped it
on his foot
OWWW!!!
So he said
I give up
I'll keep
my bad
luck.

Scott Schaffer :: Grade 4
John F. Kennedy Elementary School :: Hastings

Spring Cleaning

I yelled to the broom "get to work!"
    He did too.
    He swept faster than any broom this
    side of the Mississippi.
I looked under my bed.
    There were 2 shadowmen, 5 octopi and
    27 cacti.
        I found my mosses and fungi project
        that I had been looking for, for four
        years.
My brother was under the bed too.
    He was fighting off my pet dragon, Spot.
        So I forgot about under the bed and went up to put on
        my brother's clothes.
    I was scared stiff to look in my dresser.
        My mom always hates it when my chimp calls
        his war cry when I open my dresser.
So I skipped that.
    I went to my bookcase.
        I got trapped in a book where
        I became the main character.
So I skipped that.
    Then I thought, "Well, I can make
    my bed."
        Joke's on me.
I forgot how to because I hadn't
made it in four years.
    This was the day I got nothing done.
    My mom's voice, when she yelled at me,
    was decible 55.

I told her, "I tried. I found my brother."
This was the day I got virtually nothing done.

Brandon Ulstad :: Grade 5
Madison Elementary School :: Madison

Flying Stars

In the poem I am writing
hands reach for flying stars
that fly onto the floor. "What
a waste," people say. "Pretty soon the
skies will be dust!" So if you
find a flying star take the motor
off of it.

Joe Oxendale :: Grade 2
Zanewood Elementary School :: Zanewood

Dream Time!

One day I was jumping on my bed when my mom came up and said: Stay in your room until I say you can come out. I went into my closet and fell asleep. I dreamed I was a princess. I lost my crown and I needed it by 12:00 midnight for the Ball. I called the prince and he said: Stop and think about where you left it. So I did. And I remembered I left it in the Ballroom. So I got dressed and my crown and I were safe. I woke up and said: Why do I have a shoe on my head? And then my mom said: You can come out and eat supper. O.K., Mom!

Tara Otterbein :: Grade 3
Cleveland Elementary School :: Fergus Falls

Changes

One night I went to bed by the silver sea. The next morning I woke up just as the silver tide was pulling in. I screamed and tried to get to my feet; but I couldn't. When I looked to my feet to see what the problem was, I saw that I didn't have feet anymore, but instead I had one large fin. Whenever I tried to move, music came out of the purple scales. Then I remembered the tide was coming in. It sounded like elephants on the rampage! However, I was a musical mermaid and I could swim. Finally the huge waves struck and started to pull me out towards the sea. I flicked my tail, and the music followed sweetly while I swam with pure pleasure. I was so happy being with my sea friends; I never wanted to leave this beautiful paradise. I swam straight into the swift current heading for the ocean so I wouldn't have to leave, but I struck a rock that knocked me out. The next thing I knew I was in my mother's arms. It was all a daisy dream. I'll never forget my adventure.

Kristine Fordham :: Grade 5
Murphy Elementary School :: Grand Rapids

How Come, Poet?

How come, Poet? Is poetry like
a shooting star,
an elephant fondling a tangerine,
or a Black Hole that pulls your thoughts
on paper? A hollow tree
that holds your thoughts, like
an ice cube that melts away words
on paper,
       Hail
          c
            o
              m
             i
               n
                g
                d
                 o
                  w
                    n
and hitting your paper,
              and
                    putting
words on it?
How come, Poet?
What is
Poetry?

Leann Okeson :: Grade 3
Hillside Elementary School :: Cottage Grove

Mr. Shoes

There was Mr. Shoes sitting by the
roadside, tap dancing gracefully in the
light of the moon. I said hello who
are you. He just kept on tap dancing
so good, just like crisp clean snow
hitting you in the face in the middle
of winter when you're hot. He started
walking away. I yelled what's your
name. He said new shoes. I
really didn't know if he was a man
or woman. He was so neat it was
hard to tell.

Patrick Broderick :: Grade 5
Gatewood Elementary School :: Hopkins

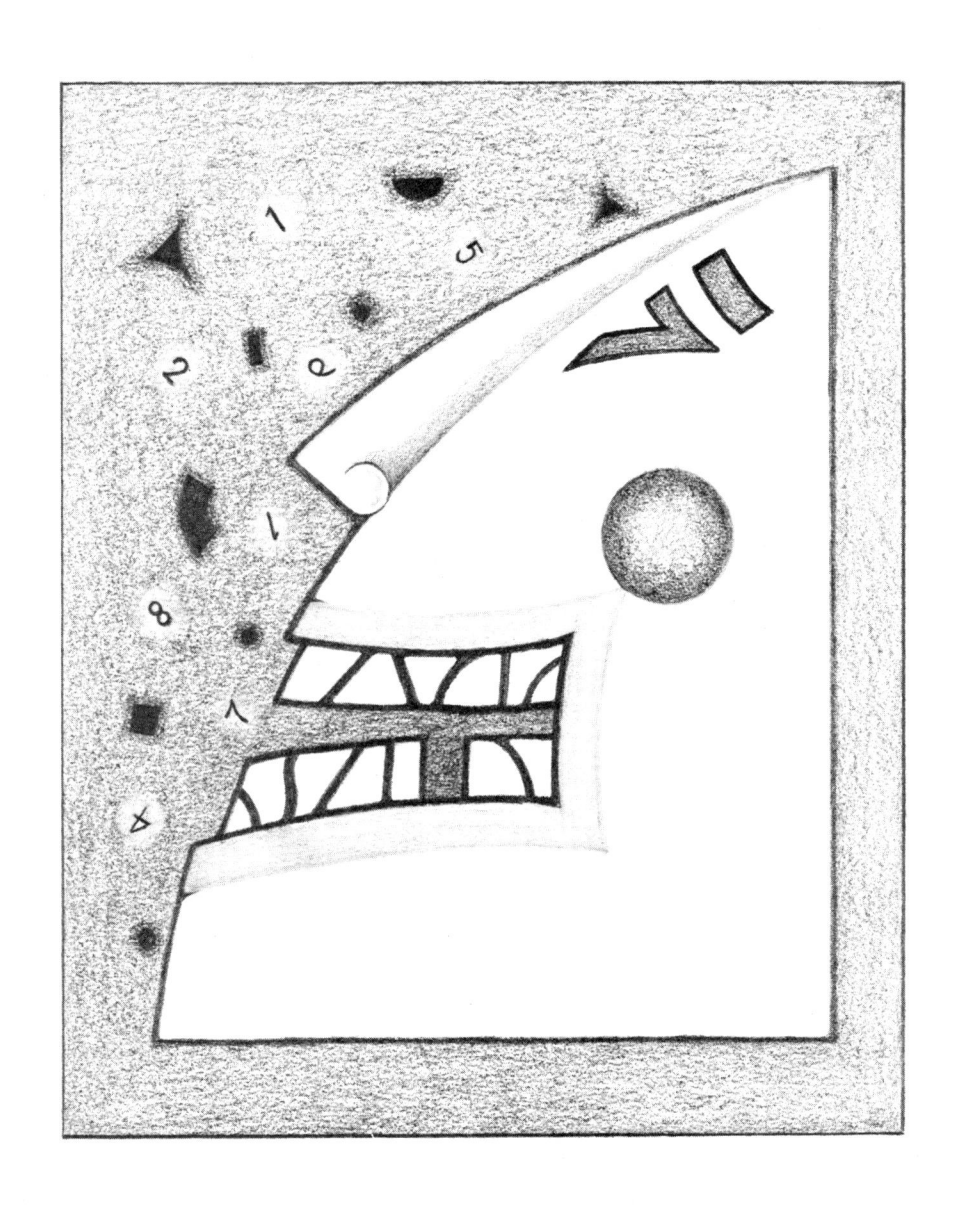

Missing a Tooth:
Growing Up

"I'M MISSING A TOOTH . . ."

I'm missing a tooth
so I cannot whistle hard.
I can whistle, though.

Katy Mikrut :: Grade 3
Lakeaires Elementary School :: White Bear Lake

History of my Writing

I remember when I first used chalk. My mom went out to buy some. I was so excited to open it and write on the sidewalks. The first thing I wrote was my address and name. Then I got older and had crayons. My mom got me coloring books. But I didn't use them, instead I used the walls. My mom was mad at me. I said I was sorry. Then it was time for school. I didn't know anything but.I asked my teacher for help. But I liked free-time. That's when I could play with my friends. Then it was time to go home. I couldn't wait for the last day of school. Summer vacation! Then I was in third grade. My brother needed a report about a black bird and I wrote a story for him but he didn't use it. That's when I got mad at him. Then I was in fourth grade—didn't do much. But then I was in fifth grade. All I did was write and learn. We had to do a report on a famous person. I chose Lincoln, two and a half pages. Then we saw a movie on Charles Lindbergh. I did a report on him.

If I was a writer, I would have a heart-shaped desk. I would write little kids books, like Doctor Seuss. I would write for the rock group called Falco. My favorite TV show is "Who's the Boss" and I would write for it.

Jennifer Talcott :: Grade 5
Pine Hill Elementary School :: Cottage Grove

A Letter

Dear Mother and Father

I climbed up a
rainbow yesterday and I saw an
elf. Then I jumped down
into a tree and I went
back to my room and read.
And the other night when
I went back into
my room I saw a
knight in
shining armor and he started to chase me
with his spear!
And last night
when you and dad were
asleep I was hungry so
I went to the kitchen
and when I opened the
refrigerator the food
began to talk!
And last night
I had a dream that you
and dad got on a boat
and went to Florida
for 14 years and I started to cry.
And I don't like it
when I get teased.
And when Tracy's room
was on fire I thought
Tracy was still in there.
And one year
ago in April when it was
thundering I slept under
my bed. And last

night I felt like an
alien from outer space.
And today, after music
I got really sick.

      Your Daughter Jamie

Jamie Miller :: Grade 2
Buffalo Primary School :: Buffalo

THE CORN PEOPLE

Here they come again,
The corn people.

Their large crippled hands
are aged ears of corn,
Their long scrawny legs
are old moldy stalks.

Their unwashed hair
is the brown rotten cornsilk,
And their black shiny eyes
are little black beetles.

When the light went out
this little three-year-old
Would scrunch up in the corner
of the good neighbor's cornfield.

Here they come again,
laughing that hideous laugh,

Glaring those beetle eyes,
threatening me.

As they draw nearer and nearer
I get scareder and scareder —
They press those jagged faces
against my only protection.

As they turn to leave
they threaten to return,
And this little three-year-old
will have to suffer evermore.

Now, whenever
I drive by a cornfield,
I get an eerie feeling;
The corn people are waiting.

Shari Briley :: Grade 8
Central Middle School :: Columbia Heights

I Remember

I know you from somewhere.
You are the boy in the picture.
It's quite obvious you're at a wedding.
I see cake, cookies, plates, punch and a large blue candle.
These are on the table behind you,
which is covered with a pretty white tablecloth
with little blue ribbons and green leaves on it.
The girl standing next to you must be your sister.
I remember now, her name is Jill.
You sure look sharp, all dressed up
in your light brown suit.
The dark brown shirt is a nice touch.
Oh, and that fancy white clip-on tie,
it's just too much.
Well, at least it matches your shiny white shoes.
So much for the outside.
Let's see what's on the inside.
Look at that smile.
I wonder what you were thinking?
You've got a far-off look in your eyes.
I remember now.
You were thinking about the future.
Mom and your new daddy.
You're pretty smart for a four-year-old.
Hey! Wait a minute!
I remember.
I've thought those thoughts once.
You. You are me.

Jack Shouts :: Grade 11
Mankato East Senior High School :: Mankato

Growing Old

Every time I smell crayons, it is 1977,
and I'm four years old. I'm in my grandfather's
dusty, old, green house, sitting next to a table
drinking the lemonade he made once a month. I'm
coloring in the color book my mother and her six
brothers and sisters used when they were young.
I'm even using the same crayons. Crayons
in a rainbow of colors: pink, brown, red, orange,
green, yellow, white, black, purple, and everything
in between. The crayons aren't working. They're
too old. The wax won't give me any color. My hand
goes limp, and I drop the crayon. I yell to the
other room where my grandfather and my mother are
discussing what should be done about my grandmother,
who has been sick as long as I can remember. My
mother replies that they're too old, just too old.

Emily Larson :: Grade 7
Highland Park Junior High School :: St. Paul

Old Motor Oil

Every time I smell old motor oil, it is the late '70's, '79 to be exact, my dad is under our old '71 Volkswagen Squareback, and I am sitting on a box in the corner of the garage. My father has just finished doing something on the engine. He is kneeling under the car pushing, straining, trying to get the engine back in. The engine is bright with a new muffler. It smells of old motor oil, black, dead, and dull. My father is dressed in an old army outfit, smeared with grease, reeking of gasoline. I help him by bringing tools. He says, "Stefan, see if you can find the 13 mil and hurry!" I run to the workbench, the workbench that is a cluttered mess, and I can't find the tool. He comes and gets it himself. I feel embarrassed that I couldn't find the tool. He runs inside to answer a phone call and my mom gets mad because he gets grease on the door. The repair on the car works, because we keep it for a few more years, it's reliable. I remember the smell of old motor oil, because it's so dead, dull, gone.

Stefan Reuther :: Grade 7
Fred Moore Junior High School :: Anoka

Garage Attic

I climb up the ladder that leads to the loft
in our garage and I peer over the trapdoor opening
and see the dust laid thick on the floor.
I hoist myself up and notice the grotesque paint job
that I was once so proud of — green and brown
and yellow verticle stripes.
Posters hang by nails, the single lightbulb is bare.
Small pieces of carpet are fitted together
like a disorganized jigsaw puzzle.
The stench of wet wood and sawdust still
lingers in the air. The light from the cracked
filthy window falls on the floor
in irregular shapes, and I think to myself,
I once loved this place?

Mike Haugh :: Grade 10
Cretin High School :: St. Paul

The First Snow

One morning I woke up,
looked out my window
and saw snow.
I jumped into my clothes,
ran downstairs and outside
to make a snowman.
I loved him and the winter
and the snow.
I came back to tell my mom,
twirling around the house.
Sailing into the kitchen,
I grabbed a carrot
and some blueberries
for his nose, mouth, and ears.
I found two popsicle sticks
for his hands.
My snowman was perfect.

Kris Kuehlwein :: Grade 5
Royal Oaks Elementary School :: Woodbury

Review of Life

I was born on September 9, 1970.
When I was small I would bring a chair
right next to the T.V. and watch Match Game.
I always used to wake up early on Christmas mornings.
It was a hot day when my favorite team the Lakers
won the championship.
It was a blizzard the day my head hit the floor and
was knocked unconscious.
I remember being on a swimming instructor's back
deep in the water feeling I was going to die.
I used to use my bed as a Garbage Truck.
I was ten when I put the croquet ball through my window.
I was hit by the ball in my first baseball game.
When I was five I cut my face after I fell off my bike.
I was very young when I ate poison berries.

Robb Gag :: Grade 9
Stillwater Junior High School :: Stillwater

School Hall Floor

I am hard with footprints.
My heart is paper and dust
swept away day after day.
I overhear kids talking
about the two who got in a fight,
about the one who told off
the teacher nobody likes,
or about a girl who changes her best friend
for the tenth time this week.
I have the most interesting people
walk on me.
I wish I was a kid
doing anything I want with my life.

Troy Wallin :: Grade 7
Willmar Junior High School :: Willmar

WHAT LIFE IS ON SALE

School is like an endless store,
Me looking through the keyhole in the door
Year after year,
Looking at what Life is on sale for me.
Maybe next year I'll come back with the key.

Ben Kuchera :: Grade 5
Lincoln Elementary School :: South St. Paul

A New Basket

COACH (C) & JESSICA (J) on the basketball court.

C: I hope you're just practicing.

J: I am. Why?

C: Because that's not right.

J: I'm trying a different way.

C: I hope it will beat the "TANS" next week.

J: Oh, it will coach. It will.

Sonia Tatroe :: Grade 4
St. Croix Catholic School :: Stillwater

From a Boy to a Girl

I don't know how
to tell you this:
I am Halley's Comet
and you are Earth.
I circle around,
I try to tell you —
But my fear draws me
closer to the sun.

Brandon Koontz :: Grade 4
Highland Elementary School :: Columbia Heights

SISTER

Don't be a big bully. Do not lean against the
wall. Don't listen to the boys. *But I don't.*
Oh yah, what about Adam? Always say please and
thank you. *I do.* No you don't. *I do big
sister.* Make your bed after you get up.
I do big sister. Do not say yes to every
date when a boy asks you to come with him. Don't
lean back on your chair. *I don't dumb sister*
Do not say dumb to anyone. *But you are dumb.*
Do not take candy from strangers. *I don't
brat sister.* Never say brat. Wipe your mouth
after every meal. Never ever drink and
drive. *I am not old enough anyway. Bully.*
I told you not to say bully. *Do not.* Do too.
Do not. Oh yah you do. You just said it.
Well you are a bully. Do not chew with
your mouth open. *Can I get a glass of water?*
I am not done yet. Always wash your very
own clothes. Why? Because it is polite. *So
who cares.* Do not kiss a boy when he wants
you to. *Why not? The boys call me kisser girl.*

Christine Touhey :: Grade 3
Groveland Elementary School :: Wayzata

The Girl

Oh, one day I wanted this girl
with the curl down the middle of her
face. But my best friend
took her away.
Oh, what a day. Oh, how I wanted
this girl.
One day she came to me. My
legs were turning to jelly
so I ran away.
The next day I found a note
in my locker. Then my friend
made fun of me. Then he ripped
his pants laughing. Then she
thought he was a nerd.
Oh, how she wanted me.

Kevin Pellersels :: Grade 4
Warba Elementary School :: Warba

Teddy

There he sat, his one good button eye
peeking out over the edge of the bag by the back step.
That familiar face, with all of its patches of fur
and the black nose dull from time.

I ran in—shocked—and looked at Mom accusingly.
She tried to explain: I was too old now
and it was time for him to go.
I didn't listen.

My mind drifted back to that first day I got him,
and all of my tears that had collected on his face since then.

Kim Haselius :: Grade 8
Central Middle School :: Columbia Heights

A Loss

Little girl
opening the box.
Anticipation;
A quick patter
then jump.
A small grey
kitten
skitters across
the room with
deep green eyes
wanting to be loved.

A tearful whisper.
the girl grown
older, remembering the
anticipations and
quick patters,
longing,
wanting to be loved.

Jodi Morgan :: Grade 11
Rosemount High School :: Rosemount

My Bedroom

The large bed is like a sick
old grandfather. The big
brown headboard, his pride
and stubborness. Every time
the bed moves, it creaks.
Every time grandpa moves
he groans.

The walls are grandma.
They too have wrinkles.
The light blue paint is peeling off
the walls. Grandma is
forgetting more and more
every day.

The two large sturdy dressers
are the parents.
Always there, never moving.
Solid as rocks.
But like parents, they're
getting scrapes and gouges
with age.

The TV and stereo
are the son and daughter.
Just flip a switch and
out pour their personalities.

They are the fun ones of the family.
They have their bad days.
The TV screen is blank sometimes

and the stereo doesn't always
have good music coming out of it.

My bedroom is like a family.

Jenifer Schoeberl :: Grade 10
Rush City High School :: Rush City

SISTER

I am the electric train, you are the track
Sometimes I run all over you
And you shock me with your electricity
But without each other, neither of us works
You supply me with electricity
In real life the electricity is love

Sometimes I derail
But I haul myself back on track
Sometimes your path is bumpy
And static keeps us apart
But the real power is in your heart

Wade Jensen :: Grade 6
Birch Grove Elementary School :: Brooklyn Park

Gift

Mom buys me a new shirt.
It looks like it came from
a Hopalong Cassidy two hour show
I watched about five years ago.

I put on my "Thanks" mask,
I think the going is getting easy—
then Mom tells me we are going
to my relatives for lunch.

She says I should wear my new shirt.

I'm thinking, "Mom
should I wear cowboy boots and hat?
Have a long strand of grass
hanging out of my mouth
and say 'Howdy' when I walk in?"

Jerimy Erickson :: Grade 8
Richfield Middle School :: Richfield

My Great Old Uncle

There were two boxes
of empty cartridges next
to the old chipped up
steps you got to take your
time now don't hurry
it he would say just
take your time aim and
blast it old drummer will
get what's left

No, no, no not that
way don't rush it
his face became as
hard as stone but in
his eye there was a little twinkle saying
you're almost there kid
you're almost there.

Howard Johnson :: Grade 7
Coon Rapids Junior High School :: Coon Rapids

"The Final Draw"

The face-off will be held at center ice in less than one minute. The most death-defying part of the game, overtime, begins soon.

The horn sounds. The noise sounds about 10 times as loud as it really is. The fans are cheering wildly. The score is 3–3.

I'm in the net. I think to myself, I must be strong, I must be strong.

The puck is in play. It hits the sticks of many players as it glides around.

Everyone is tense. Suddenly one of their team members gets a one-on-one with one of our defense. The defenseman trips, and with an "ugh" he falls to the shiny, white ice. It's terrifying!

I've always been able to handle breakaways before. But this was different. The whole team, the whole game depended on me. I would decide if we would stay in the game or if we would, well, if we would lose.

A droplet of sweat dripped down my nose. I was set in position. I looked him straight in the eye for one last second before the move he and I had to make. I felt like a deer and he was a wolf looking each other straight in the eye before the final chase.

His white skate blades seemed to glare as he cut the ice up, leaving a trail of destiny behind him. He was fast, faster than most.

Then he made his move. He swerved to the left, then swooped to the right. I moved with him like a gun pointing at his moving target. Only he was the gun, and his target was the net behind me.

Steve Munson :: Grade 9
Richfield Junior High School :: Richfield

Chicken

I came to see a concert he was in.
A recent revelation
from an outside source said
They were going to prom.

Before, to avoid the fact,
his letters covered his chicken
feathers with elusive whitewash.

I felt a ton of bricks on my chin
as I looked at Her,
But I kept it up with a shaking smile.

He left just before the concert.
"He's gonna be late" I heard,
as someone gave me his instrument.

I got away from them
and my mask slid like warm
stage makeup melting.

I retouched my mask and waited
in an empty hallway.
He ran up the sidewalk with
an unleashed smile.

When he saw me he
stuffed it into a hurried look,
the rose he got for Her
hidden also.

Guiltily he walked quickly past,
not seeing his viola.
I asked with a triumphant smile,
"Would you like your viola?"

I saw three of his feathers
fall off as he walked away.

Marjorie Ellickson :: Grade 11
Jefferson Senior High School :: Bloomington

Development

A photograph of brilliant colors and faces
    so many glossy finished faces
Yet I am still the negative,
    unclear, backwards and far
    from the final print.
Hold me up to the light
    it shines through me
    as I absorb knowledge.
You can begin to see my shape
    transfer my image,
    transfer my shape onto Kodak paper.
Allow me to write, to speak
    and you begin to see my color.
Soak me in developing fluid,
    drench me with your insight,
    help me become confident
    of my changing spirit.
Rinse and cleanse me with water
    I need time to reflect
    on the fears of developing
    the collection of images
    I now project.

Rachel Weaver :: Grade 11
Edina Senior High School :: Edina

We walked, We ran, We Flew

We walked proud and free
like great birds of prey from the city of angels
true followers of a perfect idea
pure from the city we fell away from them
We played our games of
love and war across the heated asphalt
Hoping to never touch the heated ground
We ran mischieviously
and sang of dragons who puffed
magic smoke while we were being
swallowed by a boa constrictor
We plotted easily in the lazy spring heat
devious immaculate plans that
were quickly devoured by light's real reality
Finally it came the day of our transforming
we flew farther from the city of angels
and into the broadening new darkness
like thieves in the night but knowing
there was nothing there except what
we took with us.

Dave Parkin :: Grade 10
Anoka Senior High School :: Anoka

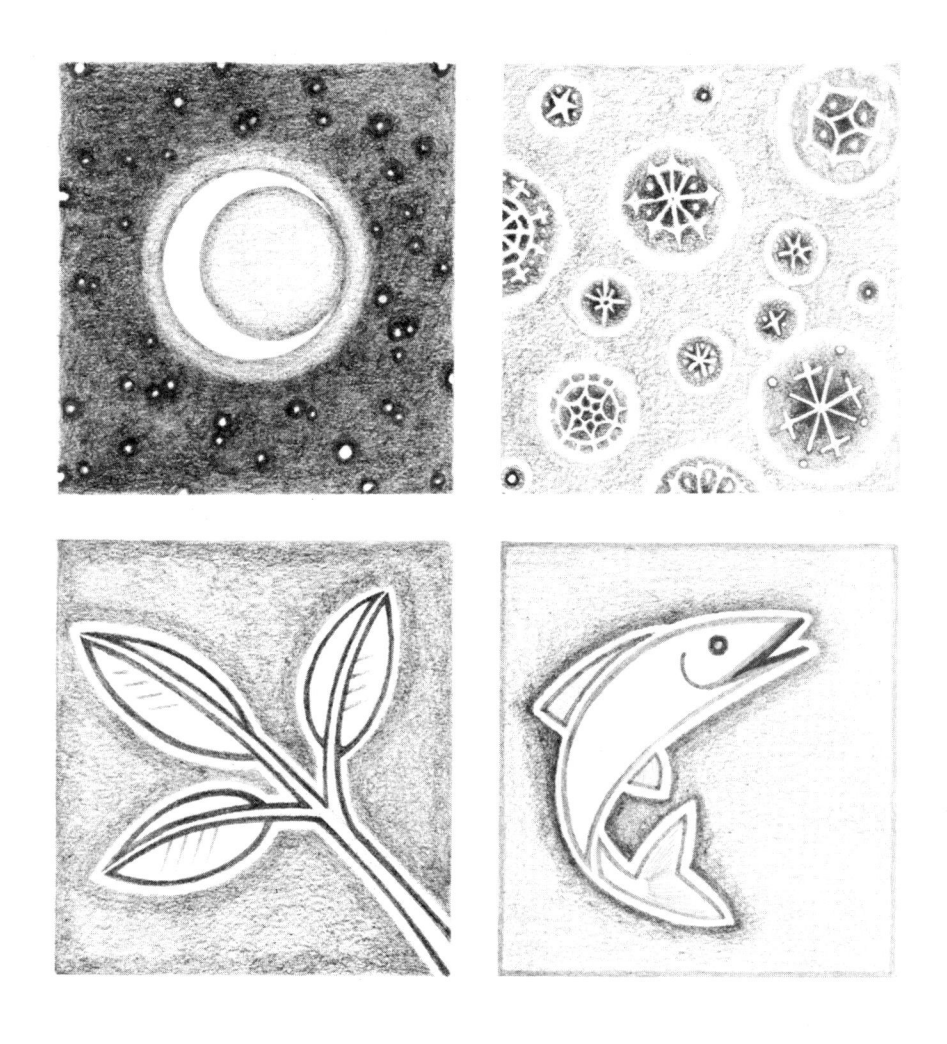

To Be With the Weather: Nature and Seasons

TO BE WITH THE WEATHER

Flying with the wind would be fun.
To go through clouds with icy droplets
sticking to your face. To fly up a mountain
and go down in the rain. To see the sight
of a tornado clutching a house and throwing
it off into never ending space. To see the
sight of a hurricane causing tidal waves
and tremendous floods that simply drowned
a house. Sighting a dust storm in the
desert blowing sand all over the place
would look outstanding. Watching a
blizzard causing huge drifts would be
fantastic. In a cool breeze or huge
thunderstorm. In a warm or cold front
I don't care. Just to be in the weather
that is my life.

Matthew Streit :: Grade 4
Holdingford Elementary School :: Holdingford

Seasons

There are many dreams in seasons
Fall is a shotgun in slow motion
shooting a fluorescent red and yellow bird.
Winter is silent — a deep, black hole
you are stuck in for life.
Spring is all seasons put together.
And summer is pepper falling on us,
burning our skin to sandpaper.

Nichole Boegemann :: Grade 3
Belle Plaine Elementary School :: Belle Plaine

OATS IN A PAIL

I want to tremble with the river
when it flows like oats out of a
pail.
When it goes past a cherry tree
I see the ruby blossoms of it.
The water is like clear tea.

Sara Kubera :: Grade 4
Holmes Elementary School :: Rochester

THE SQUIRREL

The dog was barking like
a door slamming. It was barking
at a squirrel that was stomping
up a tree. When it was gone,
it was silent. The wind whispered
like a person. The squirrel stepped
down from his nest that was
like a little pile of hay.
Then it was noisy again.
The dog started barking, the wind
started howling. The squirrel
made a magic day.

Eric Humble :: Grade 3
Rushford School :: Rushford

Trapped

I'm tired of what's right
and wrong in life.
Be polite, don't play in
the mud, do what's expected
of you. I'm tired of my
busy schedule, I have no
time for fun. Work seems
to own me. Sometimes I
wish I belonged to the
wild, the forest, and
ran wild and free like
a mustang or a jaguar.
I'd run so fast work
and death couldn't
catch me, and I'd live
forever. But instead
I'm trapped
in the eye of a hurricane,
struggling to get out. Death
will catch up, and soon
only my spirit in the
wind will remain.

Jacinda Brinkman :: Grade 6
Zachary Lane Elementary School :: Plymouth

Excerpt from "My Special Place"

I silently rode up the hill slowly letting Tandy graze every now and then. As we rounded the rustic old cider house I watched the old orchard spread in to view. I lightly eased Tandy into a slow canter up the slope. After I'd gone about one hundred yards I slowed her to a walk. I looked down at her pale creamy-colored mane and tail. They matched beautifully with her golden coat. I then scooted her over to the shortest tree around. I gently stood, carefully crouching just high enough in the saddle to reach the closest limb. I quickly grabbed for the two nearest ripened apples. Hoping I wouldn't lose my balance, I slowly settled myself in the saddle. As soon as I bit into the crisp apple Tandy swung her head around and looked at me with longing eyes. Reluctantly I held out my last juicy apple on the palm of my hand. She took it quite tenderly just like a young lady. I laughed lightly at her gimmicks. She nibbled at it, then purposely dropped bits in the long stems of grass just for the pleasure of finding them again. . . .

Jennifer Timmer :: Grade 6
Fergus Falls Middle School :: Fergus Falls

World Beyond My Home

Outside the door and warmth of my firm red house
the snow approaches.
It surrounds us, snow is not evil.
It sparkles as the early morning
breathes golden light.
Nothing moves — even the pines stiffen as we pass.
In the distance, a dog is wailing into
the echoes of silence.
Life continues in this strange place.
The stabbing, swift wind is the traitor.

Laura Jasper :: Grade 10
White Bear Lake Senior High School :: White Bear Lake

Ode to a Snowstorm

Green spruce trees standing alone
shrouded in a mist of white.

When snow comes tumbling down it looks
like little ballerinas all dressed in white.

The screens are taken to the inky blackness
of the closets to be replaced
by the powerful storm windows.

Black and yellow snowmobiles running
for their lives across the barren fields
of cold white winter.

Designs of crystal fit for a queen
covering the windows and sparkling in
the morning sunlight.

Snow is the shining goodness of a crisp
clear winter morning.

Soon snow will melt away to leave
behind the memories of another winter.

Elliot Doren :: Grade 6
Farmington Middle School :: Farmington

The Black Winter Waters

I remember black winter waters, I remember all the water of the ponds and lakes and streams, they are all frozen but beautiful and shiny like diamonds, like crystal shining in the summer sun. It feels like frosty silk
                        covering a
                        wooden
                        template,
                        the little
                        pieces of
                        frost look
                        like pieces
                        of cotton
                        out on a
                        shiny piece
                        of glass. At
                        night out on
                        the water you
can only see blackness and the dimness of the moon shining on the calm shiny waters. The ice sheet on top of the water is a sheet going over a bed. A cuddly blanket soft, smooth, and nice.

Ben O'Brien :: Grade 4
Woodbury Elementary School :: Woodbury

Winter Extravaganza

Listen to the crackling of snow
under children's feet.
Dress in warm clothes.
Watch the snow floating like leaves
to the ground.
Feel the ice under your blades,
as you skate.
Serve a hungry bird a chocolate nut.
Salute the big bare trees.
Hear the snowmobile whizz like a race car.
Watch the cars slide across the ice.
Dream of spring coming like a snowstorm.

Sara Rose :: Grade 5
West Elementary School :: Worthington

Spring

Spring is the best season.
The birds come back.
The train hops into town.
The flowers come alive,
sing to us. They start
break dancing.
The school runs away.
The children
flow in the rushing
water and start
tweeting.
The grass buzzes
and plays music.
The kites come alive.
All the planets
are dancing.

Collaboration :: Grade 2
Olson Elementary School :: Bloomington

A Likeness

I'm outside standing
in the rain
thinking of popcorn
popping at home—
as the raindrops
fall to the ground
with a kind of sound
like pop, pop, pop
as if popcorn were
popping on the ground—
and see the rain
splash to the ground the same as butter
falling on the popcorn.
As the rain stops, the
big puddle like the
bowl of popcorn is
filled, as the sun comes
out and covers and takes
away the water, like
I'm opening my mouth
and making the popcorn
disappear, but as little
raindrops lie on the ground
little pieces of popcorn
lie on the table.

Adrienne Feske :: Grade 4
Thomas Edison Elementary School :: Moorhead

ON SHREDDED WING

On shredded wing, a butterfly
fights to remain aloft, tossing with
unseen currents.

On shredded wing, a butterfly
climbs, higher . . . higher . . .

On shredded wing, a butterfly
triumphs . . . only for an instant.
On shredded wing, an unheard sigh
as life ebbs away.

On shredded wing, a butterfly floats . . .
endlessly . . . into forever.

Mark Olson :: Grade 9
Plymouth Junior High School :: Plymouth

Distances of Nature

Here out on the lake
with waves sometimes lolling
sometimes deep and rough,
the ever-changing, ever-broadening sky
bends gently down
touching the water's edge.

There is life in me as well as in the sky.
At times these lives touch.
Other times they are as distant as the planets.
I am at your mercy
moving the way you move
and shining the way you shine.

When I am calm I show off your ecstasy,
but when I am angry
I heed not your warnings, brother.
I am not always of your blood.

Dan Knudson :: Grade 11
Battle Lake High School :: Battle Lake

A Picture of Me

I am sitting on the grass.
The grass hurts because I'm sitting on it.
The grass is twisting away from me.
The wind is screaming.
The wind is making the clouds cry.
The trees are twisting their branches
to wipe the clouds' tears away.
And I am smiling
on the outside.

Shawn Clitty :: Grade 6
Jefferson Elementary School :: Alexandria

"Faith wasn't . . ."

Faith wasn't a real pretty girl but she wasn't ugly. She had long red hair and freckles all over her face and arms. You could barely see the freckles because of her dark tan, but she knew they were there. She had a wiry frame, but she was strong. Anyone who worked on a farm all their life had to be strong.

The farm was a great place. The huge red barn took up most of the area. Then came the house, the chicken coop, the stables and the corral. This was the farm, except for 100 acres of crops that surround the place. And one solitary road that leads up to the highway. Of course she couldn't forget the old wood fence that surrounds the whole living area. That fence had been there for years.

Many generations had lived there starting from great, great, great grandfather to Faith.

Faith lives here all alone now. She had one brother who came by once in awhile to help with the hay. Between him and the horses, the farm was all she had.

Shaking her head to clear the sentimental thoughts, she walked to the barn. She had the funny feeling of something awful about to happen. Well, whatever it was she would be ready.

She walked over to the barn and went to the loft. The sweet smell of fresh cut hay filled the loft. A sharp whinny broke through the air. "I'm coming Bessy," she yelled. She ran over to the stables. She spread the hay carefully but quickly. Her freckled face and red ponytails bobbed as she hurried. She went outside. She took a long look around. The tall, erect buildings stood solemnly. She ran her hand along the rough, splintering fence post. After the storm this would be gone. Then the harsh winds of a tornado began to blow.

Melody Hanson :: Grade 9
Bemidji High School :: Bemidji

"I SAW THE ROCK . . ."

I saw the rock in the field under plowed corn
caked with mud and stiff clay.
It whispered to me like the moon riding the wind,
     the purple lizards crushing it with impunity,
the lichen growing on it, destroying it,
     the yawning earth ingesting it,
          and the red light of the ground warming it,
the pressure of tons of "friends"
crushing part of it away.
     It told of the brown midnight it was vomited
          out of the ground
to live another thousand years without friends.
Could this be our life.
     I left the rock to be lonely for another thousand years.

Tom Juenemann :: Grade 10
Woodbury High School :: Woodbury

The Nature Day

The meeting with sun and nature.
Picking up leaves without burning
ourselves. Eating the raspberries and
climbing trees to the top just like
you were touching the sun.
And playing in the leaves. "Ouch," said I,
pricked in the eye with a leaf.

Brian Sontag :: Grade 5
Lincoln Elementary School :: Detroit Lakes

"I'M THE ONLY CHILD . . ."

I'm the only child
outside. I can feel
the wind as it
hits me, it reminds
me of lots of flowers
in a field.
It smells like sweet
cinnamon. It makes
me think of the fun
I had at my grandma's.
Some guy stares
at me like some rope
tied around him.
I still think
I am the only one.

Tina Kassler :: Grade 4
Forest Lake Elementary School :: Grand Rapids

GREAT-GRANDFATHER

At seventy-seven years,
he should not have been
pumping that water.
His eyes gleamed at the
fresh water trickling down
in pearls.
Spotting a lady bug
on the pail,
he looks at it carefully,
and watches it move gracefully
across his rugged hands.
My great-grandfather
is so peaceful as he works.
Trimming the hedges,
he measures the height
by the touch of his hand.
He finds a baby robin,
and tries to help it fly
back to its tree.

Greta Raduenz :: Grade 8
Shakopee Junior High School :: Shakopee

Essence

My eyes open to the blooming earth,
its hands reaching up to the sun.
I walk upon its roots
and the grass engulfs my naked feet.
The warmth seeps through
the ominous pine trees as
they drink the juices of the sun.
A crow calls my name in
darkened pitches of verse.
I hear the sounds of
the earth growing,
growing into sunlight.

Amy Derr :: Grade 9
Northview Junior High School :: Brooklyn Park

The Shinto Gates

The old man walks down
a garden path,
oblivious to the world of evil
outside the Shinto gates.
He stops for a moment
to contemplate a hibiscus flower
growing at the side of a waterfall.
For hours he walks on
witnessing a beauty, nature.
When he returns to the gates,
he would like to stay
but leaves without sorrow
or hesitation.

Chris Nordby :: Grade 6
Afton-Lakeland Elementary School :: Lakeland

The Deer

I once saw two deer:
a buck and his companion
leaping through the underbrush,
their faces
like two frightened children,
fleeing and bouncing onward.
With gracefulness
they kept their ears erect
and bounded away
with their slim legs;
over the ground,
over fallen leaves, stones,
around the old trees,
through thick patches of grass
they fled
like a roaring river,
like two runaway slaves.

Sue Durand :: Grade 11
Prior Lake High School :: Prior Lake

The Large Sky Reaches Down:
On Living

Volcán Irazú
Largest Volcano of Costa Rica

The stench of sulfur
fills our nostrils.
Pumice crunches underfoot,
black as night, yet light as air.

The wind roars.
My friends and I laugh, singing
"Sacrifice for the gods!
But who shall we throw in?"
The steam hisses in reply.

Down in the crater,
a bubbling yellow lake
is angry with motion.
Miles away
to either side
lay two wide, blue oceans.
Salt air dances along, steam
making curious patterns,
dancing in my hair.

The large sky
reaches down and touches me.
Clouds fly by.
Where do they go?
How do they dream?

"Time's up!" cries the guide.
We start back,
walking a trail of sand
with memories of a place

destructive and beautiful
like life.

Charles McGuire :: Grade 11
Cretin High School :: St. Paul

The Beaming Light

I am the heart of the Earth.
I dream to make the world bigger.
I guess I am just a beaming ball
of flames,
but I serve a good purpose.
I listen to myself make mountains.
I change landscapes,
make new and peaceful land.
Some people regret me,
but most don't.
When I sleep, I listen to rocks melt.
Much of my life is spent
working on the landscape.
I never saw humans
except I feel the weight
of big pyramids on top of me.
I know I didn't make them.
So it must have been humans.
I think that's what they call them.

Adlai Czarnomski :: Grade 6
Goodview Elementary School :: Winona

Mom

Mom, you are the strength
of my body. I am only a horse
running wild and free, the wind
blowing through my mane.
You caught me and now
I am your child
and you are my mother.

Danae Meyer :: Grade 3
Chosen Valley Elementary School :: Chatfield

Laos to Thailand

Running in the forest where
the trees and plants are colorful
with yellow and green.

Me, crying with fears. Communists
are right behind us. We have been running for
forty days and nights from the country of
Laos to Thailand. My uncle, carrying a two
year old baby, he was carrying me.

I'd cried because I was starving. I
remember it all from a baby to a boy.

Boonpheng Kavanh :: Grade 5
Hawthorne Elementary School :: Rochester

THE LIFE OF A DOWN'S SYNDROME CHILD

—for my Buddy—

In the bed of fright, he laid wondering
mysteriously what the fruit basket of
tomorrow would include. Was the laughter
and mocking only an imaginary motion,
or would it be reality of the coming day?
    No one knows.
    But the gray color of thunder rolls on in his mind.
    Over and over
    All through the songs of night, he thinks of
his ever so protective sister. She soars watching ever
so carefully, and the wind which she soars in is full
of love for him. If the taunting was brought
to life, would the heartbeat also begin in her fist?
    No one knows.
    But the gray color of thunder rolls on in his mind.
    Over and over
    Before he knows it, he is awakened into the
day of alteration. He can tell by the golden stars
of sunlight, beaming into his hesitating eyes.
Should he rise even with the anxiety? Or should he phony an
unknown disease and stay
in his large world of wonder, not knowing
what adventures that day would hold?
    No one knows.
    But the gray color of thunder rolls on in his mind.
    Over and over
    As he walks to the door of the unknown,
he kisses his beaming sister once more, good-bye.
He was now on his own, in a world of dreaming
children. Dreaming children, soon to be simplified,
realistic adults, or at least older people.
As he walks in the busy, spaghetti-like highway

of the classroom, he sees a girl, eyes full of salty pools of tears. He walks over, smiles, and the fun-filled childhood friendship began. The rest of that day, that year, and the year after that was fine. No teasing or taunting. The boy's smile kept its beautiful dreaming shape. But as the children got older, would the mocking begin?

No one knows.

But the gray color of thunder rolls on in his mind. Over and over.

Katie Eichten :: Grade 6
John Glenn Middle School :: Maplewood

Poem With Refrain

A little bird entered
my heart and heard
a rainbow playing a harp.

Everyone lives in my heart,
it wakes me up with a start.

A bunny rabbit jumped
into my eyes and saw
burning diamond rainbows.

Everyone lives in my heart,
it wakes me up with a start.

A bumblebee fell
into my mouth and said,
do you have any money?

Everyone lives in my heart,
it wakes me up with a start.

Bonnie Jo Snidarich :: Grade 3
Sand Creek Elementary School :: Coon Rapids

"Billy Hotchkins lost his cat . . ."

Billy Hotchkins lost his cat.
I see it turn south down West Main Street.
It's a black and white, very scared male
with a large red gash over the left eye
where Billy's sister hit him with a rock.
He walks past cracked windows
with yellow tape on them.
Past Rexall with its dirty carpet
and elevator music.
Inside a teenage girl buys diatac.
Billy Hotchkins lost his cat.
He runs past youngsters parking their bikes
on the sidewalk
and pelting each other with Skittles,
past cigarette butts
and bare brickwalls
with old gum stuck on.
Past an elderly couple
and a voluptuous lady jogger
in blue Adidas shorts
listening to her headset.
Billy lost his cat.
It runs past walls with peeling white paint
and an old man with a pot belly, overalls
and red cap
taking his grandson in the dimestore.
Past an old worn penny lodged
in a sidewalk crack.
Past a red Volkswagen
with one tire on the curb.
Past dented green garbage cans
with the inscription "Keep Your City Clean" on them.
Past the midget from KMCA radio
and the store with the chimes on the door.

Past Mrs. Peterson from the daycare center
with a group of pre-schoolers.
And past the Orpheum Theatre
with its smell of buttered popcorn.
Billy's poor cat runs wide-eyed
to the end of the sidewalk,
stopping just in time,
nearly being hit by a yellow Falcon
filled with loud kids and louder music.
Suddenly he is lifted by small hands.
The cat turns and nuzzles the boy's dirty neck.
And purrs.
Billy found his cat.

Bryan Eggen :: Grade 12
Ada High School :: Ada

SILENCE OF THE EARTH

The earth moves silently like the sunrise.
The oceans roll like thunder in summertime.
Volcanoes silently burst in the night.
Clouds drift like angels.
Wild animals run silently through forests.
Rainbows fall to the earth, like dust.
Silence is the hole earth is constantly falling into.

Chad Meiners :: Grade 6
Caledonia Elementary School :: Caledonia

LIFE

My life is a hawk with no feet.
It cannot feed itself.
It can't even stand on its own.
On the ground it is helpless, yet it can fly.
When it flies, it is glorious,
But the landings are bad.

Matt Schlotthauer :: Grade 8
John Adams Junior High School :: Rochester

The Shark

The shark is the teacher of the blue sphere.
The pupils do not learn this,
They know.
The shark is a graceful politician.
The issues are never expected
Or unexpected.
The elections come in frenzies.
There is but one voter who can change
the outcome.

Jon Shankland :: Grade 12
Grand Rapids High School :: Grand Rapids

The Fierce Lion

He lives on a throne looking for wonder like
a bone. His eyes are so golden and his teeth are
like gravel on a hot summer day with only
one sandle. His hair is so soft and his crown is
made of dried up corn, like his father when
he was born. And his sons sit on his back
while he's looking for food. And his queen is
sitting on his throne knitting a sweater made
out of bones. And that is the life of the
fierce lion.

Mandi Thoemke :: Grade 5
Pullman Elementary School :: St. Paul Park

The War

These little stars jumped
off the flag and sunk
into my skin.
Then the stripes wrapped around me.
The stars had tiny pins.
They stabbed my organs.
The stripes twisted
around my arms and legs
and squeezed so hard
I couldn't breathe.
So I dropped dead.
After a while, a man found me.
I don't know who it was,
of course.
The flag was lying
by me,
so the man put the flag
on my chest.

Shawn Petersen :: Grade 4
Northern Elementary School :: Bemidji

When The Moon Sails Out

When the moon sails out
the silky, shiny, slinky gowns
are put on
and the make-up is applied
in front of
a mirror.
When the moon sails out
the brass doorknobs
are turned,
to allow the pristine
to come in and socialize.
When the moon sails out
the small wooden skiffs
drift over the silent
waters.
When the moon sails out
the grimy hands smelling of
fish and musk
grab hold of the rim
of his tiny craft
to steady his departure.
When the moon sails out
the wealthy sit and shine
silently sipping the aged ale
and talk of higher-class things.
When the moon sails out
the paint chips away from the dock
as the man comes in
from a long day of work.
When the moon sails out
the giggles
are frequent
with the help of the vintage.
The money flies from hand to hand.

When the moon sails out
the old man walks on the
cobblestone street
and feels the jingle in his
pockets that can't equal two bits.
He looks through the window
of the saloon
to catch a glimpse of
them.

Jenni Adams :: Grade 9
Hosterman Junior High School :: Plymouth

The Hammer

The hammer is like a jackhammer
breaking up the concrete for rebuilding.
The hammer is a bat hitting the ball and
making a homerun.
I am bigger than a nail as I hit it into wood.
I am smaller than Reagan who is
starting a war.
I grow angry like a bright red tomato
blooming in the garden.
I make houses and buildings with
my hammering power.
I shout like an atom bomb blowing up
a country.
I want to say stop building homes
and taking all the forests from loving and
caring animals.
I want to say we should stop fighting
and killing.
I should be like a loving person.
I should be peace.

Paul Welch :: Grade 6
John Glenn Middle School :: Maplewood

Keep on Living

Sometimes when I'm laying in bed I think
Why do we go on living?
Living with screwdrivers that have been dropped
    in our milk
Living with questions about why thermoses
    keep things cool and hot
With cameras that grab your hair when
    you try to take a picture
Don't waste your time wondering about
    why George Washington was the first
    president
And as you lay in bed don't wait for
    death to tap you on your shoulder
Instead go on with your life —
    walk across the ocean
    be the first person to walk to Jupiter
Don't cry out "I want to call up Death
    right now!"
Instead wait till it comes your way
In the meantime
    Put up with the boogey-monsters.

Jodi Sommerfeld :: Grade 6
Zachary Lane Elementary School :: Plymouth

Winter Skin

This is for those who fear to die
yet have not been born
Life is you, reaching for the sky
Your Father shaking Uncle Sam
by the hand, Mother singing
in the shower
    Every day is now
    Every year was then
"Breakfast's on the table, boy"
"It's cold out"
Lined and crackled apple mother
serving me oatmeal with her fingers
I'm outside
first breath after the warmth of home

Che Regnier :: Grade 9
Worthington Junior High School :: Worthington

I wake up and remember . . .

sleeping in a house in a foreign land
whose little lizards climb the walls
blowing bubbles and lighting firecrackers
with my grandfather
driving down the streets in town
seeing sights I have not seen since
people everywhere
buying and selling
fish, shoes, toys, shirts
the smell of frying food
going back to sleep again
under the smell of the mosquito coil
and the insect net . . .
I wake up and remember . . .

Robert Atendido :: Grade 8
Oltman Junior High School :: St. Paul Park

A Teacher Taught

There was a teacher who taught the sun.
One day the teacher taught the sun
how to get hotter and hotter.
She taught the sun to get so hot
she burned up!

Tim Gustafson :: Grade 2
Rockford Elementary School :: Rockford

The Sun

The sun is a hot ball of fire
                 a red rose
                 a star
and when it stops to think it sees an ocean
and wants to take a swim.

Jason Moudry :: Grade 6
New Prague Elementary School :: New Prague

"I am just a kid . . ."

I am just a kid
making a living in school,
I don't learn — I think.

Jason Surface :: Grade 4
Riverview Elementary School :: Grand Rapids

"Because our minds . . ."

Because our minds are so drunk
with dreams, some of these dreams
are shattered. Our minds
start to drift into ideas with
greater detail and a whole new
mist of dreams develops. While
all of this dream shattering
and rekindling is going on,
time is chopping away
like an iron hoe.

Tom Prow :: Grade 10
Woodbury High School :: Woodbury

Ode to the Planets

The planets
are like
balls you
can play
with by
kicking them
and passing
them and
bouncing them
on top
of each
other and
by bouncing
them like
a basketball.
They are
like floating
maple tree
leaves and
some planets
have rings
and they
are like
hundreds of
planets floating
around other
planets and other
planets and
even more.

Then sometimes
they're like
falling snowflakes
calling out to

help catch
them.

The moral of the
story is we should
cherish what we
have.

Bobby Withers :: Grade 4
Swanville Elementary School :: Swanville

"Every day the sun . . ."

A: Every day the sun goes down with those same warm colors. I never miss it unless the clouds won't permit it.

B: Yes, but when the light's gone, then it gets dangerous.

A: There's nothing here after dark that wouldn't be just as dangerous in the light.

B: But they can see better at night than we can.

A: Who's they? Nobody has been here for years. Just animals.

B: You can stay but I'm going home by myself!

James Peeders :: Grade 8
Fergus Falls Middle School :: Fergus Falls

Deer

A deer, a graceful deer, is like a seed
blowing across the meadow where
wheat is as yellow as a one month
old chicken that has been hatched from
an egg in the red barn, big as a school.
I go into Rushford where children
go to learn and play, but a fawn just
born stands on her sturdy legs
like a piece of wood that has been cut
in the mill. A little baby fawn is running
through the forest with its mother
who is big and strong like a cow grazing
in the grassy land. Where animals
gather to be fed, a baby fawn,
when it runs, it runs as fast as the
squeaky mouse that woke me
up at night in my bed. Why
can't I hear like a deer
in the silent night? Why can't I
be a deer?

Adam Rislov :: Grade 3
Rushford School :: Rushford

My Friend the Moon

I have seen you
with the Sky and Stars
and with the night.
I have seen you with the wind
and the weather — and
in the shadows. . . .

You chase them away from me.

Seton McCool :: Grade 5
Washington Elementary School :: Thief River Falls

Writers in Residence

The following writers conducted COMPAS Writers-in-the-Schools residencies during the 1985–86 school year:

Paulette Bates Alden
Sigrid Bergie
Bill Borden
Michael Dennis Browne
John Caddy
Alvaro Cardona-Hine
John Fenn
Margot Kriel Galt
Phebe Hanson
Ellen Hawley
Dana Jensen
Bob Kearney

Patricia Kirkpatrick
Roseann Lloyd
John Minczeski
Kathleen Norris
Nancy Ortenstone
Nancy Paddock
Ruth Roston
Bart Schneider
Richard Solly
Susan Marie Swanson
Mark Vinz

The efforts of these creative and dedicated people is what makes the COMPAS Writers-in-the-Schools program vital and valuable. They have earned our thanks and congratulations for the work presented in this book.